T0147145

MAALIYAH RUBEN

authorHOUSE®

AuthorHouse™
1663 Liberty Drive
Bloomington, IN 47403
www.authorhouse.com
Phone: 833-262-8899

Published by AuthorHouse 10/20/2022

ISBN: 978-1-6655-7405-1 (sc)
ISBN: 978-1-6655-7415-0 (e)

Library of Congress Control Number: 2022919703

Print information available on the last page.

There was a mother, Sarah Whitlock, and a father, Oliver Whitlock. A mother of light and love, and a father of hatred and darkness. The two fell in love over the bond of magic. They had a baby, Aria Whitlock. The two raised their baby girl to the age of sixteen. She had begun to show great power, the older she got. Along with Aria showing greatness, her father started to distance more and more, he was eventually presumed dead after disappearing for eight months. One day, Sarah took Aria out to the town, not knowing that this was the beginning of a horrific circumstance. Walking down a shady ally to get home in Leicestershire, England in 1992, men of three appeared. Their faces covered with masks, and hooded robes, the middle man pulled out a wand and struck Sarah into death; meanwhile the other two hooded men grabbed Aria with great force and put her to sleep.

Three days later she awoke in a place of concrete, and chains. Not knowing where she was, Aria assumed it was a prison, but she didn't understand what for. A door opened and came through a man, she didn't know, asking her what she remembered. Aria had told the man nothing and acted confused, but deep down she remembered everything. He gave her a meal and some water, continued to silently watch her eat, then left with nothing spoken; this shall repeat for a week. Later another man showed up, Aria asked him politely to use the restroom. Given there was a window in the restroom, the man made Aria leave the door open, but as she sat down she noticed something in the man's pocket. It came quickly to her that it was a wand. She gently pulled it out and tucked it under her shirt, into her pants. Up came the moonlight, she assumed it was time for these men to rest their heads. Aria pulled out the wand, not knowing any spells for her circumstance, and concentrated extremely hard on what she wanted to happen. Suddenly, the chain on her ankle quietly bursts from her skin. Off she went through the window she had dreamed of escaping for the past week; she ran as far as she could.

Aria found herself wandering the woods next to this prison trying to figure out where she was. It looked like home but something was different. She looks around and discovers her hands tingling. Out came a bright burst of light. She points toward a tree, and it almost feels as if she can pull herself to the tree. She wondered what would happen if she tried to point her hands to the ground and pull. She slowly and unsurely pointed her hands to the ground. She then tugged and felt herself get shorter. Aria then decides to yank herself down, curious of where she'd go. She appears to be in the same spot, but the prison is gone. She recognizes the smells and sounds around her and realizes she is home once again.

Aria wanders the streets of her hometown trying as hard as she could to gather her thoughts. She visits her home and gathers the things she would need for a fight, in a panic-like state. She took a photo of her mother with her; she left in a hurry. Aria's goal was to find another wizard who could teach her how to protect herself. She finds the nearest library where she hopes to find peace and information. Aria sits down at a table across from a gentleman wearing all black, pitch black hair, and a black cane. They find each other continuously looking back and forth at each other. She wonders if he knows who she is.

"Sir, excuse me?" she says with loneliness in her eyes.

"Yes?" he replies"

"Would you happen to know who I am?" she asks with curiosity.

"No ma'am," he suspiciously replies.

The man gets up and walks away, leaving behind a paper. Aria grabs it and tries to find him, but of course he is nowhere to be found. She then finally looks at the paper; she notices it's an address and a map. Aria waited awhile before she came to the thought of finding this place, hoping to find the man. It takes her two days to find the place on the paper. She decides to rest for that final night before reaching her destination. Woken by the warmth of the sun she gets up and keeps walking. Aria looks up from the paper to find a castle-like building. She is amused but yet she still feared for her life, as she saw what happened to her mother Sarah. Aria walks up to the building and goes inside. The first thing she notices are all the children of mixed ages. Next, being the robes and hats the adults are wearing. Aria wanders the halls of this place until a wise gentleman walks up to her quietly.

"Can I help you?" he asks.

"I'm looking for a man, in all black actually. He left this paper behind at the library. What is this place?" she asked with confusion.

"Well this is a school of wizardry. We call it Watford School of Witchcraft and Wizardry. Maybe it wasn't such an accident he left that behind eh?" he says with a chuckle.

Aria proceeds to smile nervously.

"How did he know I-"

The man cuts her off.

"A wizard can always identify another struggling wizard, Miss Whitlock. Now, Tell me, where are you from? We've never heard of a Whitlock wizard family before," he says seriously.

"Well, I've always known I was a witch, my father disappeared one day, so we just assumed he passed away. My mother, on the other hand, was recently murdered by a wizard. I'm not sure who, or why, but I need to know how to protect myself. I think something is coming for me. A few days ago something strange happened. I was in a prison. I managed to break free but there was something strange about the place. Can you help me?" she pleaded.

"Hmm, I think I can figure something out for you here. Do you know how to use your powers?" he asked.

"Just for small things, sir," she said.

"I am Professor William Longtail. It's a pleasure. I will allow you to take some classes and will introduce you to a man I believe can help you with exactly what you're looking for. Come, follow me," he requested.

Aria followed Professor Longtail down a long, dark corridor. Finally stopping at a door with a plack that lists "Professor Burton."

"This professor teaches offensive and defensive strategies. I believe he is exactly what you're looking for, and could possibly teach you some things you did not seek to learn, but will be grateful for. Let us introduce you." Professor Longtail states.

They walk in a massive square classroom, dimmed lights, and a bit of a chill.

"Welcome, Professor Longtail, what can I do for you?" says Professor Burton.

"Yes, hello. I have a young girl here who will be needing your assistance. She needs some more, let's say, advanced strategies. I assume I can trust you with this professor?" he asks.

"Well of course you can, she will be in great hands," Professor Burton said, smiling from ear to ear sarcastically.

"Well then, let's get you a robe. Do you happen to possess a wand Miss Whitlock?" he asks unsurely.

"Just this one I took from the guard at the prison, sir," Aria states.

"Well that wont do. I will have one delivered to you by morning. In the meantime Professor Burton, please show Miss Whitlock where she will be staying until further notice. Give her something a little more private. I presume she has a lot of thinking to do," Professor Longtail sympathetically articulated.

Aria and Professor Burton talked for a long while into the night before she was finally shown her resting place. She started putting the few items she brought along on a small table next to her bed. She couldn't stop thinking about her mother and what happened to her. She stared at the photo of her mother for hours throughout the night. Suddenly she felt the tingling in her hands again.

Aria dropped the photo immediately, having no clue what it meant. Why here? Why now? She wondered. She didn't want to risk anyone finding out about what she could do, not just yet anyways. She laid her head down, gently closed her eyes, and slowly drifted off to sleep.

"Until tomorrow," she uttered.

The sun began shining bright in the sky once again. However, Aria is still asleep; awoken by the sound of pounding on her door.

"Miss Whitlock! Miss Whitlock! Open up, it's time to start the day. I need your assistance with something. Come find me when you're more, should I say, conscious," Professor Burton stated.

Aria then got up and started getting dressed. First her shirt, then her pants, and then her robe. She had nothing to comb her hair, but it was still braided behind her head from the night before. She splashes some water on her hands and rubs the top of her head to make her hair flat. It doesn't work as well as she hoped it would. Walking away from her room, trying to find Professor Burton's classroom, she finds herself lost. She walks with a quick pace, bumping into a stunning middle-aged woman.

"Oh my gosh, I'm so sorry! I'm trying to find Professor Burton," Aria says.

"That's okay, no worries. I am Professor Nona Bliss. Nice to meet you, Miss?" Professor Bliss questioned.

"Whitlock, ma'am," Aria replied.

They gracefully shook hands.

"Follow me darling, I will take you to his classroom," offered Professor Bliss.

They took a long walk all the way to the other side of the school. Professor Burton standing in the doorway. He then proceeds to carefully watch over Aria as the clock spins to the end of class. Every once and a while she would watch back at him. No student has ever examined Professor Burton the way Aria had. It had caught him off guard every time. It was such a familiar feeling, and he didn't know what to think of it.

"Whitlock!" he says, as he summons her.

"Yes professor?" she replied.

"We need to start your training. Would after dinner be okay?" he asked

"Yes, that would be amazing, thank you professor," she said.

The rest of the day went pretty quickly for Aria. Finally dinner came along. She still had yet to introduce herself to anyone besides the professors, until one student finally came up to her.

"Hey, I'm Collin Reed. What's your name?" he questioned.

"Hi, my name is Aria Whitlock. It's nice to meet you," she said.

"Thank you, it's also a pleasure. Did you just start going to school here?" he said.

"Kind of, I don't really go to school here. I'm just here to do some training and then I'll probably have to be on my way. I'm not sure how long this training thing will take," she replied.

"Well, if it's not an issue I'm always here if you need anything, or have any questions about anything. Sometimes this place can be quite stressful, sometimes it's just nice to have someone to talk to who isn't authority," Collin says.

"Thank you, I will definitely take advantage of that," she says with rosey cheeks.

Aria finishes her dinner and realizes Professor Burton never told her where to meet him. She finds her way to his classroom and he isn't there. Next, she tries to find her way to the nearest courtyard there, and finally standing there, heavy eyed with his arms crossed, Professor Burton.

"Hello professor, I'm sorry, I wasn't sure where you were. I went to your classroom but you weren't there," she pleaded.

"Yes, that's my fault, but never be late to training again. If you're as worried as you say I don't expect that to be a problem, is that correct?" he asked with an attitude.

"Yes, that's correct," she reassured him.

"Alright, well, first things first you need to show me what you're already capable of. Can you do that?" he questioned.

"Yes," she replied.

Aria began to show the professor all these amazing things that no one else at the school could do. For example, she could communicate with animals of all kinds. Second, when in fear, she is able to read the mind of the person endangering her, giving her an advantage to sense their weaknesses. Last, but not least, she can repair any broken magical object with her bare hands. She had the instincts of a goddess.

"Well, I don't think this will be as difficult as I thought," Professor Burton said with a genuinely confused and frustrated look on his face.

"Thank you, I'm glad to hear you say it professor," Aria replied.

"These happen to be extremely rare gifts, if you're not already aware," he said.

"Really, I wasn't aware. I assumed these were things all witches and wizards could do," she replied confused.

"No Miss Whitlock, they are not. I am going to have to, as you children say, crack open a book, about these powers of yours," Professor Burton said.

"Okay professor, I have some things I'd like to take care of as well. Please let me know when we can begin training again," she said.

"Of course," he replied.

Aria walked around the school searching for Collin.

"There are so many people here I'm never going to find him" she says to herself.

"Find who?" Collin says as he appears from the crowd.

"Oh, hi, I was actually looking for you," Aria says with a startled chuckle.

"Well, tell me what you need," he says.

"Okay, let's sit. I have this ability, if one should call it that, and I'm not really sure what it is or what it means. Look, you can't tell anyone but, these beams of light shoot out of my hands and whichever direction I'm pointing my hands, well I can travel there. When it's about to happen I can feel my hands tingle and it's really bright," she informs him.

"Wow, that's uh… amazing Aria. I don't even know what to say. I've actually heard about this before. It's extremely rare, but we'll have to read more about it before I give you the wrong information," Collin replies.

"Well, I'm not exactly done yet. You see, before I came here, I was imprisoned. There was a field of woods next to the prison, and when I escaped, this light came out of my hands. I pointed them toward the ground and started pulling myself down and I appeared to be in the same spot, but only the prison was gone and I was back in my hometown," Aria said.

"That's interesting, let's head to the library," Collin suggests.

Aria begins following him down these massive corridors, and a big red door meets her eye. Collin struggles to open the door.

"This door may need a little oil," he nervously says.

Aria chuckles at the unflawed clumsiness of Collin. They get through and it appears that nobody else is there, but that seemed to relieve Aria. The two searched and searched, but could not find anything about what was going on with Aria. She throws down the last book she tried to read, Collin sensed her frustration. He glanced at the book she threw.

"Are you kidding me?" Collin yells.

"What? What is it? Aria replied.

"This is the book we have been looking for the past two hours! Let's see what it says," he stated.

They moved close together, both reading at the same pace.

"Oh, my God. Are you seeing this? It says, your power is called 'speed traveling', this allows you to not only travel at amazing speeds, but also through other dimensions. This must mean that prison was in another dimension," Collin states.

"Wow, this is insane," Aria replies.

"It says that anyone besides the person who possesses this power will be blinded if looking at the beams of light, as well as anyone who tries to touch these beams of light could die," Collin informs.

"So, does this mean that I can't show this to anyone?" Aria asked.

"I assume that's correct, but I suppose if someone were to have a magical pair of glasses, they could probably watch if not join you," Collin says.

"Okay, I'm going to ask Professor Burton if he can manage to make something of that sort up. If he can, I'm going to show him this power, and maybe I could show him the prison I was being held at," Aria enthusiastically says.

"Well, good luck with that, if you need any help just, find me," Collin says flirtatiously.

Aria speeds through the halls, racing herself to Professor Burton's classroom. She finally gets there.

"Professor, may I come in?" she asks.

"Why of course, what can I do for you?" he questions.

"Well, I wanted to tell you, I have one more ability that I have not shared with you yet. I can only show you at night, when everyone's asleep. No one can follow us, no one can see. There's only one condition," she states.

"As if you are in any power to list any condition to me, go on, what is it?" Professor Burton asks.

"Well, I sort of need you to make some kind of glasses. They need to be so strong that if wearing them you could stare at the sun as long as you wanted with no harm done, sir" she replies.

"And why might I do that exactly?" he asks.

"Well, you asked me to show you, that's why you will do it. Unless you don't want to see," Aria says with frustration.

"I'll get right on it then. I've seen you have introduced yourself to one of our students. Are you comfortable with him?" the professor asks.

"Yes, he's actually the one that helped me figure out all the rules of this ability. I actually just came from the library with Collin," she said.

"Good, I am going to ask him to be your mentor, so if you are feeling lonely, or curious, you shall go to him. If he cannot answer your questions, I will be your next resort. I don't want you to feel scared to tell me anything. I am here to help you through whatever crazy nonsense you're going through," Professor Burton says lovingly.

Aria nods her head and goes to find Collin. Professor Burton on the other hand has trouble making these glasses. The more strategies Professor Burton tries, the more he fails. Becoming more and more frustrated, he comes to a realization. Is he starting to care for Aria? In fact, is he starting to love her like his own? He does not know where these feelings are bubbling up from. He feels as if he and Aria represent a future. A professor with dark hair, an all black suit and robe, and definitely a dark attitude.

Then comes along a caring and brave young lady of lushes, dark, locks of hair who actually pays attention to him, but also is not afraid to stand up to him. He hasn't felt love like this in a long time. He feels as if he has found family, once again. Professor Burton finally finds a mix of materials that will allow him to do what Aria asked of him. He finds himself feeling peaceful, and for some reason seeking her approval.

Collin felt the urge to give Aria a tour around the school. He showed her the classrooms, he was very excited to spend time with her. The Mythological

Creatures classroom, where you learn about all sorts of creatures such as dragons, unicorns, and phoenix's. Next, they walk down to the Concoctions classroom, where they learn how to mix certain ingredients for magical results. Last, but definitely not least, the Charms classroom, where they learn different variations of spells. Aria and Collin make their way down to one of the back courtyards, Collin pulls out his wand and out comes a radio playing a romanticized unflawed melody.

"May I," Collin asks, sticking out his hand.

Embarrassed by Collin's gesture, Aria grabs his hands as they slow dance, slowly letting her head rest on his chest. Mesmerized by the compassion and love Collin is willingly showing to her, she sheds a tear near the end of the song.

"Hey, whatever it is you're going through, don't forget I'm right here by your side, and I intend to stay. We haven't known each other long, but I can already tell you possess a heart of gold. Who wouldn't wanna be around that every second of every day. Just know, I will never, ever, forget the day I met Aria Whitlock," he says with passion covering his face.

"When I found out I was going to be staying here for a while I never pictured it like this, but I can surely tell you, Collin Reed, that you have been the best host, and I feel the same way. Thank you for standing by my side with no questions asked, so far," Aria lovingly chuckles.

As Collin and Aria have their moment, Professor Burton slowly approaches.

"Hello, love birds, may I speak with Miss Whitlock in private for a moment?" he asks.

"Of course sir, come find me when you can," he says to Aria.

"Hi professor, what's going on?" Aria questions.

"Yes, I just wanted to let you know that I was able to figure something out with these sunglasses you asked me for. I wanted to know if you were feeling up for tonight, or if you would like to wait until tomorrow evening?" Professor Burton asks.

"Um, yes we can go tonight, but are you sure they will work? I don't want anything bad to happen to you.

You and Collin have been the only two people I have been able to connect with since my mother passed and I-" Aria is cut off once again.

The shocked but subtle look on the professor's face when he hears Aria saying this. He was filled with joy hearing that someone could actually love and care for him.

"You're spiraling Miss Whitlock. Do you trust me?" Professor Burton asks with confidence.

"Well of course I do, but I also care about you professor. When we first met, you scared me. You have such an intense character, and as you know one of my abilities is being able to tell the weaknesses of those I fear, even just a little. When I saw your fears, it made me sad. I don't want you to fear those things anymore, and I will do what it takes to change them even if you push me away. I don't want you to feel alone professor," Aria stresses.

The confidence in Professor Burton's face instantly disappears. He stares silently at Aria.

"I will meet you in my classroom after the students and remaining staff are in bed," Professor Burton strictly says.

Anxiety rushing through Arias veins, she watches Professor Burton walking away with his head to the ground. She runs up to him from behind and as she crashes into him, tightly locking her hands around his abdomen. He slowly turns around and starts hugging her back. All the students and staff in the audience of their moment with petrified looks on their face, stand frozen, wondering what it was about her that finally broke Professor Burton's hard streak. This was something they have never seen before, and they're not sure if they ever will again.

"By the way professor, your mind is now safe from me, I no longer fear you," Aria says with heart.

Professor Burton smiles at her, gets up, and walks back to his classroom. Aria follows him inside and wanders a different direction. She slowly paces the corridors examining every little detail she can. She hasn't felt the feeling of home in a while, but this school starts to really grow on her. As it's time for dinner she goes and looks for Collin once again. Instead she comes to find Professor Bliss.

"Professor Bliss?" Aria says.

"Hello Miss Whitlock, how has your training been going so far, I trust Professor Burton is taking good care of you. That was some kind of hug. I can't even remember the last time we've come close to seeing him like this, you must be very special to him" Professor Bliss states.

"Well that's actually what I wanted to speak with you about. I was wondering, why does he act so grumpy, and so closed off to everyone. I'm sure if everyone saw him the way I do, they'd think so differently of him, and maybe he wouldn't feel so alone, do you know what happened to his family?" she asks.

"Well Aria, he wasn't always like that. Back in our more prime years, Professor Burton had a daughter. Her mother got sick and passed away early in life. His daughter attended our wizardry school, and there were boys who thought they were playing around, just teasing her, and they accidentally casted a curse upon her soul. It killed her. Those boys no longer attend our school. I assume Professor Burton was reacting quite normally at first, but then he never changed. I guess he just assumed that living life would be easier if he didn't truly care about anyone. He would never have to lose them," Professor Bliss responded.

"Wow, I can imagine what that must be like. Maybe that is why we connected so quickly, we both lost our only family. I feel so sorry for him. Does he ever talk about this? What was his daughter's name? Aria questions.

"His wife's name was Mary Burton, and his daughter, Alexia Burton. He doesn't talk about this darling, but what we saw today at school, I can't say he wont talk to you about it," Professor Bliss winks at Aria.

"Thank you professor. Really I am grateful you trust me with this," Aria says.

Aria finally finds Collin and they sit together and start eating their dinner.

"I have an idea, let's sneak out tonight. There is something I wish to show you," Collin asks.

"Well, I don't think I'll get in much trouble either way, but will you?" Aria questions.

"No, I do it a lot actually," Collin says.

"I can't tonight, maybe tomorrow?" says Aria.

"Of course, just come find me when you can," he insecurly states.

Aria walks back to her room. Looking out her window once again waiting for all the others to finally fall asleep. She can't help but feel numb. So many things running through her head at once. All the memories, good and bad. Replaying her mothers death and her fathers disappearance, next to Professor Burton and

Collin. Aria starts hyperventilating. Physically feeling her heart shatter into pieces, she lets out a cry.

"NO! Why is this happening? I can't do this!!" Aria screams.

She starts pounding and punching the walls, knocking everything over. She flipped her bed, there was not one thing in the room that hadn't been tossed or penetrated. Of course that same night it happened to be Professor Burton's night to patrol the corridors. He hears something toward her room and instantly panics. Running as fast as he can, he finally gets to her door.

"Aria!" Professor Burton shouts.

He runs into her room as she lets out one painful, and unbearable scream. Professor Burton can't even wrap his head about what happened, or why her room looked the way it did. His face is filled with fear, shock and empathy as he listens to Arias' broken cries.

"It's gonna be okay, please listen to me it's gonna be okay," Professor Buron tells her.

They sat in that same spot as she cried for hours in his arms. Aria then got up, picked up her wand, and finally casted a spell on her room to clean itself up.

"Let's go," Aria tells Professor Burton.

He curiously follows her through the halls, but can barely keep up with her as she sprints her pain away. Running to the spot where she first was when she got out of the prison, she finally stops. She lets Professor

Burton catch his breath as she knows he was having a hard time following her the whole time.

"Put the glasses on," Aria demands.

Professor Burton puts the glasses on.

Aria looked straight into his eyes, being able to show him her pain, she put her hands out as if she was holding something. She screams, and throws her hands up as fast as she can, letting out beams of light into the starry night sky. It feels as if everything is moving in slow motion for the professor. Almost as if he is terrified of Aria. She looks over after she finishes her terrifying scream, to see Professor Burton's face, realizing she just did something godly.

"Grab my waist!" Aria screams.

Professor Burton grabs Aria's waist. He is terrified. He watches as she slams her arms down as hard as she could. They quickly start rising and it doesn't feel as fast as it looks, but it's like a lightning bolt to the naked eye. They get to the dimension with the prison and she immediately looks for the professor and jumps on him with her hand over his mouth.

"Don't. Say. A. Word. They are aware I am gone," Aria demands of him.

Aria stands up and sees the prison. She focuses as hard as she can trying to see if she is close enough to the guards to see their fears, because of course she is fearful of being found. She could read every guard's mind if she wanted to. She stops, and looks at the professor with the most fearful look he's ever seen, and he looks back.

"They're all scared of the same thing," she utters slowly.

"What?" Professor Burton questions.

"Do you know this place, professor? We're in another dimension," Aria states.

"No, I've never been here before, Aria why didn't you tell me right away that you could do this? Do you know how rare this is? Can your parents do this?" he questions, never losing his composure.

"My parents couldn't, and I didn't at first, but Collin helped me learn more about it and how to use it properly. The things it could do to people. I could kill anyone with this power professor," Aria claims.

It's finally time to go home and start Aria's real training. She takes Professor Burton back to their normal dimension and they walk back to the school together.

"Aria, please come see me when you have some time tomorrow," Professor Burton pleads.

"Okay professor," Aria says, with the most broken and scared look on her face.

"Hey, look at me. I said we're in this together. Please don't forget it," he states.

They both finally head to bed after an extremely eventful night together. Neither of them could sleep that night and they can definitely see it on each other's faces the next day. Aria woke up and did her morning routine, after that she headed to Professor Burton's room. Today something just happened to be off with her but she told herself she would push through.

"Good morning professor," Aria greets.

"Hello, how are you feeling today?" Professor Burton questions.

"I'm fine, can we get started on training soon please?" she asks.

"Of course, meet me in the courtyard after dinner," he says.

Professor Burton could tell something about her was different. He wasn't sure if it would wear off or if this was the new Aria, seeing that's how his past also was. Professor Burton started to get really frustrated. On the other hand Aria decided to go speak to the wise Professor Longtail. She went to his office to see if he was there, as he knew she would. He welcomingly greets her inside.

"Please Miss Whitlock, have a seat. Is there something troubling you?" Professor Longtail asked.

"Yes actually. I need some help with something but I'm not quite sure how to ask, professor," Aria states.

"Well just ask," he says with a smile.

"Well, as you know, my father was presumed dead after he didn't come home for eight months. I just need some help finding some stuff out about him. I'm having a hard time believing he is dead. I wanna try to find out more of what happened when he first disappeared. Do you think you would assist me with this?" she hesitantly asks.

"I can certainly try. Why don't you and Collin go to the library and try seeing if there may be anything there about your father. I suppose anything that has to do with wizards and magic should be in there. Also I need to inform you that you will be starting classes very soon. How is your training going with Professor Burton?" Professor Longtail asks.

"It's going alright sir, but I have noticed something. Out of all the people I've met since I have been here, Professor Burton is the only person in which I don't know his first name. Why?" Aria asks.

"That is a good question Miss Whilock. You see, when it comes to Professor Burton, he likes privacy. I overheard you speaking with Professor Bliss, so I won't stretch this, but he will only share his first name with those he really trusts. The ones he has grown any sort of attachment to. When his daughter first passed away, he couldn't do anything but blame himself. What he would have done if he would have been there. He is an extremely powerful wizard, but I believe he would like to be treated as any other, and that says a lot," Professor Longtail replies.

"Okay, thank you sir. So, when I'm not training, and I'm not doing classes just yet, what is there for me to do?" Aria asks.

"Well I'm sure your friend Collin shall be missing you. Maybe see what he's up to, and see if there is any information on your father. Come back to me and let me know," Professor Longtail said.

Aria goes to find Collin, but she feels as if she is missing something. Instead of going to see Collin she goes back to her room instead. Searching everything in her room, even though not much can be seen, she discovers the picture of her mother has gone missing. She's very upset but not surprised considering her luck so far. She starts walking down the hall, again to seek Collin, but he isn't anywhere to be found. She then goes to see Professor Burton. He is also nowhere to be found.

"Hello, Miss Whitlock?" a man questioned.

"Um, yeah hi that's me, may I ask who's asking?" Aria questioned.

"Of course, my name is Linol Steven. I am from the hospital wing. I just wanted to kindly introduce myself as I assume you must be staying here?" he asks.

"Yes I am sir, thank you and hello," Aria says.

"I wanted to ask if you would assist me in my wing today. You don't need experience. It's more of a learning opportunity. Would you like that?" Professor Steven asks.

"That sounds really fun, I would love to, professor. What kind of stuff usually happens in the hospital" she asks.

"Ah, well you'll definitely see very quickly that this is not a job for the weak stomach community. All sorts of crazy things happen. It can stretch from broken bones to sickness to growing frogs out of your skin, or perhaps having a non-stop waterfall of boogers running from your nose. The thing I love most about being in the hospital wing is seeing all our students so eager to learn even after enduring what they did," Professor Steven says.

"I bet there's a lot of students that come here, do any of the professors ever have to come here?" Aria asks.

"Not really, our professors possess enough knowledge to usually take care of their issues on their own, but I suppose if they weren't able to figure something out, the next place they would look is to me," Professor Steven states.

"I guess that makes sense, what do you do when there is no one here?" she asks.

"One thing about the hospital is there is always someone in need of some kind of assistance. It's not common for the hospital to be empty but if it is, we usually just go about our day and see how else we can provide for the school," he replies.

"Can I just ask, do you ever feel unappreciated for your services?" Aria asks.

"Rarely, the students are very respectful. Anyways, it looks like we have our first patient for today," Professor Steven says.

As the lights in the room start to brighten a student who seems to have scales on their skin and is having a hard time breathing walks in.

"Well, what do we have here? It seems as though Mr. Winburg here was the victim of a rebounded spell, or curse should I say?" the professor says.

"What's a rebound spell?" Aria asks.

"It is when one who casts a spell or curse fails to do so and it rebounds and hits them instead of their opponent. What happened?" he questions.

"We just wanted to go swimming, and we tried making it so we could breathe under the water. We were casting each other but my friend said the charm incorrectly. Please help me! I think I'm actually turning into a fish!" Mr. Winburg pleads.

Professor Steven walks to his desks and searches for a vile.

"Ah, here it is. Drink this. It's gross but it will help you. It may take a few hours before the scales go away but you'll be able to breathe normally again. Don't go near any bodies of water for two days, otherwise you will be back here drinking this again, and I'm sure you don't want to do that," the professor states.

"Thank you sir, what's in it?" the student asks.

"This potion consists of wolverine sweat, the extremely small tooth of a fairy, and two twigs from the purest tree on the school grounds, go on then," Professor Steven says.

Mr. Winburg smells the vile and starts to gag and cough. He gives the professor a look of worry and confusion. Afterwards, he proceeds to drink the potion. He drops the glass onto the floor and starts wiping his mouth and tip of his tongue.

"Yes, that happens. You'll be alright. Off you go now," the professor says.

"That was awesome!" Aria states.

"Yes, quite. Are you enjoying your time so far in this wing? I had a feeling you would think it was quite a catch," says Professor Steven.

"I am. I feel like even though I've only witnessed one person so far this will be fun," Aria laughs.

In comes a young girl who seems to appear with mood changing skin. The professor already knows what this is from.

"This is an example of a curse that is brought upon one another and the victim's skin turns into any color of their mood. Red for mad, yellow for happy, and green for sick etc. In this case we will need to perform a counter curse. Now, I want you to pull out your wand, point it at her, and say 'Aloom Alormus'. Ready?" he asks.

"As ready as I'll ever be," Aria states

Aria proceeds to pull out her wand. As every wizard knows if you don't get the swish and flick correct, your spell probably won't be correct. She takes a deep breath.

"Aloom Alormus!" she says.

The girl's skin starts to go back to her natural color.

"You might want to stay away from the sunlight as you will burn extremely easily for the next few days," Professor Steven says to the girl.

"Professor, I'd love to stay longer but I have some things I need to take care of. If I am welcome I would love to come back again sometime," Aria says.

"You are always welcome here, I'll be seeing you then, have a good day," says the professor.

Aria walks out of the hospital wing and continues to look for Professor Burton. She makes her way down to the courtyard as they have previously arranged. Then she remembers she was supposed to go after dinner not before, but she wasn't really in the mood to eat or speak to anyone much. She just kept thinking about her mother.

She decided to sit in the courtyard all through dinner, which is an hour long.

The longer she is out there, the more affected by the nature around her she is.

The warmth of the sun, the smell of the breeze, the feeling of the touch of the grass. She sits and waits, more and more, until dinner finally comes to an end. Professor Burton begins to walk to the courtyard, but as he can see through the pillars of the castle, he can see that Aria looks distraught. He calmly walks up to her, and kindly touches her on the shoulder.

"Are you ready to begin, I'll be teaching you two spells today," he says.

"Yes," Aria replies.

"Alright, the first spell I will be teaching you is one of the more important spells. This is a protection spell. It can be used to block any curse thrown at you. Now remember, this is not an offensive spell, it will only block and protect. It will not win a fight for you. I want you to get your wand ready, and you have to use your whole heart with this, but I want you to say 'Penitrum'. Let's see what you got," Professor Burton says.

Aria takes a deep breath, plants her feet and gets her wand ready.

"Penitrum!" she says.

Unfortunately for Aria it did not work. Professor Burton has never seen this before. He tells her to try again, but this time to really consume the feeling of power. She plants her feet, gets her wand ready, and takes a deep breath.

"Penitrum!" she screams.

It is the brightest Professor Burton has ever seen the spell casted. With a frozen and shocked look on his face once again, he comes to realize she is not a normal witch with a couple of extra gifts. She is one of the most talented witches not only of her age, but in the world.

"Okay Miss Whitlock, clearly this wasn't challenging enough for you. I'm going to now teach you a spell that will help you in the darkest of times. Same preparation. I want you to say 'Flotora' okay?" he says.

"Flotora!" she says.

A bright light shines, in fact her entire wand is now glowing a beautiful bright light.

"Is it, like, a flashlight?" Aria asks.

"Yes, it is Aria. Those are your two spells for today. I want you to keep practicing when you have some down time. I also want to talk to you about something else. Professor Longtail gave me the rundown on where you are from and your family and where you were before you came here. You don't have to fight this battle alone. I will come with you, but not till we get you trained enough to actually fight someone who may be putting your life in danger.

"Thanks," Aria says with a sad grin.

"Same time, the day after tomorrow, be here," Professor Burton says.

"Okay professor," Aria said.

Alas it is time for Aria to sleep. She walks to her room, but quickly realizes she has yet to see Collin. She walks around and finds the boys' dormitories. She walks in and looks for Collin, and succeeds.

"Hey, how's it going? How did you get in here?" Collin asks.

"Get dressed and meet me in the corridor so we can talk okay?" she replies.

"I'll be right there," he says.

Collin proceeds to put on his pajamas and follow her out to the corridor. He feels nervous, as if there are butterflies in his stomach. He felt relieved that Aria came for him, he was starting to think she was losing interest.

"So what's up, what's going on?" Collin asks.

"Well I just wanted to say goodnight. I haven't seen much of you lately. Training is starting to get busy, and I have been spending a lot of time with Professor Burton and Professor Steven. I want you to know that, I still think about you," she says flirtatiously.

"I'm not going to lie, I thought you were losing interest, but I am glad you came around. I hope your training is going well," Collin says.

"Look, I'm not sure how powerful of a wizard you are, but when I have to leave to go to the other dimension again, I want to know if you'll come with me. Professor Burton will also be there but a wise man told me that if I needed help, all I need to do is just ask. You can think about-" she's cut off

"Yes," Collin replies sentimentally.

Although it seemed like everyone had been cutting her off, this time was her favorite. She gave Collin a tight loving hug. Then she walked to her room and got in bed. This is the craziest couple of days she's ever had. She's always been a small town girl who wasn't allowed to show her powers to anyone, and now she's around people who only have powers. She hopes to find Professor Burton teaching her more offensive strategies in her next training session. Aria wakes up and does her morning routine once again. She knew today would be a quiet day for her. She engages in a journey around the school, smelling the flowers, sight seeing the courtyards, and admiring the fine details of the castle. Professor Burton meets her eye and she walks up to him

"Hello professor, how are you doing?" Aria asks.

"I'm doing alright, yourself?" Professor Burton replies.

"I'm doing alright, pretty quiet day for me so far, not surprised if that'll be my whole day to be honest," she says.

"Why is that?" he asks.

"Something just feels funny. I'm not sure what it is, Hell if I'm able to even figure it out" Aria replies.

"I'm sorry to hear that, I expect you'll be on time for training today then?" he remarks.

"Yeah," she answers.

At this point in time the professor starts to see something is still off with Aria. She can usually endure his dark attitude, but today it seemed as if she was over it or didn't care anymore. He knew the feeling of having to do your job even when you are depressed and on a girl like Aria he knew it'd be tuff. He also knew that she was struggling and maybe just needed a little push.

"I have a class right about now, so I better get going. Would you like to join me and perhaps learn a thing or two? I'm covering for Professor Bliss, I have been a lot recently," he asks.

Aria accepts and follows him to his classroom. She notices how fast and stable the professor is walking.

Her eyes followed each step as he flew quickly to his classroom. Aria sits down and observes the class from the back of the room.

"Okay children, today we will be learning how to brew a potion that will allow you to be invisible for one hour at a time for each serving you drink. For this potion you will need a pinch of lilac, the slime from the bottom of a snail, and one leg from a black widow. Following, you will take out your wand and cast a spell upon your brew. You will say 'Invisibilis', now I want everyone to get started. I will walk around and grade every movement you make," Professor Burton says with a straight face.

Aria notices how differently he is in class rather than when she is with him alone. She wonders if it's because they connect really well, or if he just simply loves to scare the crap out of his students, possibly making them take him more seriously. Once she discovered what he was teaching she felt relieved, as if some of this process may actually be a good time. She notices Professor Burton paying close attention to his students. She also happens to notice the two boys screwing around. Aria is confused that the professor knows they are not doing what they are supposed to, but has not said anything yet. It's finally time to show the professor their potions and the two boys had nothing done. As a result they quickly threw whatever they had and casted a random spell on their brew.

“I see you two have already finished, I have to say I’m quite impressed,” he said.

“Yeah we’re pretty good at this stuff professor,” they replied with a giggle.

“Drink it,” the professor replied.

“Wha-What?” they questioned.

“Did I falter? Drink the potion,” he says intensely.

The boys look at each other not knowing at all what will happen to them, as Professor Burton already has knowledge of.

The boys begin to drink their potion, and as disgusted as they are, the boys start to melt in front of everyone in the class. Faces droopy, they start screaming out of fear.

“Off to the hospital wing you two go. You will also receive an F for today,” he says.

As Aria experienced this process she began to feel better about her day, as Professor Burton had hoped. Each day that went by Aria and Professor Burton got closer and closer. Aria walked up to the professor once the class was over.

“I guess I’ll be seeing you after dinner then, I hope you have a really nice day, professor,” she says.

“You too Aria, I just want to let you know I will only be teaching one spell this afternoon. This is quite a useful spell. I think you’ll enjoy it,” the professor replies.

Aria thanks him and goes to lunch. Seeing all the students together and all the professors together was really hard for Aria at times. Sitting at a very long table all by herself, Professor Bliss walks in and notices. She kindly offers Aria to eat with her as she notices Collin is not around. She brings Aria up to the table with the professors and pulls up a chair for her.

"Go on then, aren't you hungry?" Professor Bliss questions.

"Not really, I am thirsty though," Aria replies.

Professor Bliss nods her head, but strongly disagrees with Aria for not having lunch, as she has not had breakfast either. On the other hand Aria hadn't even noticed that she had not eaten anything that day. Professor Bliss takes the lunch hour as an observation period of time. She watches Aria's behavior and mood to make sure nothing bad is going on. At least if it's something she cannot handle alone. Professor Burton finally gets to lunch and notices Aria sitting at the table with all the professors. Professor Bliss signals to him to sit down next to her. Aria gets up after a while to use the restroom.

"What's going on with Miss Whitlock?" Professor Bliss asks.

"I'm not sure, she has been like this all day. I invited her to sit in my class today and it had seemed she felt better, but I guess it happened to be temporary," Professor Burton replies.

"Well, are you going to fix it?" Professor Bliss replies with a smirk on her face.

"Well, Professor Bliss, I am certainly going to try," he replies.

Professor Burton then leans close to Professor Bliss.

"I haven't told anyone about this, but since Miss Whitlock has arrived I have grown to care for her very much. She just has the same energy as Alexia. I'm not trying to make her my daughter, but I will show her how much I care for her and would do anything to protect her as I suspect she would do the same for me," Professor Burton says with confidence.

"I wouldn't doubt it, you two seem to share something quite special. Do you think you'll tell her your first name?" Professor Bliss questions.

"At the right moment," he replies slowly.

As Aria is walking back to lunch, she notices Collin walking to the same room from the opposite direction. He looks up and notices her as well.

"Hey, I've been looking for you!, Collin says.

"Yeah, me too. This school is ginormous. I barely know my way around as it is," Aria replies.

"That is very true. How are you feeling today? I heard about the other night, when you were yelling in your room. Someone in my dorm was going to the bathroom and they heard you and Professor Burton. I felt so ashamed I didn't know till I did. Don't worry, not a lot of people know about it. I made sure they kept their mouths shut," Collin sympathizes.

"I'm sorry, I should have told you. This is all just really scary. It's like, at the end of the day I'm not sure who I am going to have to fight or even kill when this is all over. What if I can't beat them, what if I lose or even worse, what if you or Professor Burton, or anyone for that matter, got hurt or killed. I couldn't live with myself," she cries.

"Aria, there is one thing you have to remember in all of this. Whoever is helping you, whether it be me or Professor Burton or anyone, are already aware of the risks we're taking. Your only job is to fight for yourself and remember that we're by your side because we love you," Collin says.

He freezes as he just realized what he said out loud.

"You, love me?" Aria asks with doe eyes.

"Umm, well I'm going to be honest, yes from what I've seen so far. I was soon going to ask you to be my girlfriend and now I'm hoping you'll say yes now that we got the whole I love you situation out of the way," Collin says laughing nervously.

"Of course, but I have something to admit, I've never been in a relationship before but I promise I will try to be a good girlfriend. I only have one condition," Aria states.

"What would that be?" Collin asks.

"Well, sometimes I get busy or make mistakes, or even forget things. I just don't want you to leave me if I happen to make little mistakes once and a while. I have already had too many people leave me this year as well," Aria replies.

"What's a relationship without a few mistakes every once and a while, huh?" Collin chuckles.

The two lock their hands thinking nothing of it. They slowly walk into the dinette.

Suddenly they hear the room go silent. Every student, teacher, and even the groundskeepers were staring at them. They were not sure what to make of it so they just stood there and stared back at them. After a couple seconds the room returns back to normal. They sit down and Aria watches him eat his food. He offers her some but she respectfully declines. Lunch had finally come to an end. Professor Burton sees Aria sitting in the corridor just watching all the students go by as she quietly dozes off into the community.

"Hey, can we talk?" he asks.

"Of course, anything, professor. Are you alright?" she asks.

"Yes, I'm going to be straightforward with you. I just wanted to check on you. You seem different today and then seeing you walk in with Collin. I want to, how do I put this, I want to make sure you're not rushing things too fast. You're going through a lot and I'm not trying to be your father but I've personally grown to see you as my daughter, in a way," professor Burton says lovingly.

"If this makes you feel any better, I will definitely tell you if things are becoming too much for me to handle.

Also, Professor Burton, you're the closest thing I have to family. I see you as a father figure, please don't think this is a one way street," Aria replies.

She rests her light head on the processor's shoulder, which he did not expect.

"There is something troubling me, well a couple things actually, but I have already talked to Collin about one of them, but the other I fear he can not help with. I saw no point in bringing it up," Aria says.

"What about me, is there any way I could help?" he asks.

"I don't think so. With both my parents gone, and if I actually survive whomever it is that I will have to fight, I'm afraid I will have nowhere to go. Maybe I should move out of the country. Or maybe even investigate a new part of ours. I'm not sure really," she anxiously replies.

"I will never, ever, let you be alone or have nowhere to go. Do you understand me?" Professor Burton demandingly asks.

She looks at him and looks back at the floor. He gently squeezes her arm and hugs her harder. Meanwhile at the prison, the so-called top wizard possessed the photo of Aria's mother. He pulls out his wand, and casts a spell that will allow him to spy on Aria through the photo.

"Exploratorium," he aggressively whispers.

He then transports the photo back into her room, in which he cannot access physically because the school has natural protection barriers and guards around it.

It is time for the second round of classes for the students. Aria still struggles with finding her place in the school so far. She thinks it would be a good time to start looking for Professor Steven once again, as he said she is always welcome. She takes her time making her way down to the hospital wing. Throughout each of her days in the school she consistently thinks about all the things that brought her to where she was. Aria continuously looks for a distraction because she's not sure of how she would react if she didn't try to keep herself busy.

"Hello Professor Steven," she says.

"Hey! Have you come to help me with the students again?" Professor Steven asks.

"Actually yes, I figured I would since my training doesn't start until after dinner," Aria replies.

"Of course, you're always welcome here Aria. It has been kind of a quiet day today, but I suppose there is always someone in need," he says.

"Professor, can I ask you something, completely off the record?" she requests.

"Um, sure, go ahead. I think that would be okay," he replies.

"I was just wondering, if you have anything to help me focus better on my tasks at hand. Whenever I'm not doing anything I tend to think about, well, everything. I'm scared that I'm not going to learn everything I should if I'm always thinking about the things that have led me to where I am right now," she says.

"Well darling, that's not really how the hospital wing works. I do have something that I believe could help, but unfortunately I won't be giving it to you. A true powerful witch, which I believe you to be, needs to learn how to set those things aside. Magic is wonderful, it is, but your character and what you do with your magic, is what defines you," he replies.

"I understand, professor. I just had to ask. I have been trying to keep myself distracted, but I don't really go to school here so there's not really much for me to do. That's actually what led me to you today," Aria says.

"Just remember what I told you Aria. Even if it doesn't stick right now, those words will eventually mean something to you, I believe you will do the right thing with my words to you as well," he replies seriously.

The next thing you know Collin shows up at the hospital wing. It seems as if he has twisted his ankle.

"Collin? What are you doing here? Are you alright?" Aria questions.

"Yes, I'm fine. I think I twisted my ankle. I fell off my broom. Just felt like a little joy ride and then all of a sudden boom. I was on the floor," Collin informs.

"Is there something we can do for him, professor?" she questions.

"Well, if there wasn't I don't think I'd be employed here anymore," Professor Steven chuckles.

He walks over to his cabinet of potions and grabs the potion in the middle.

"Here, drink this. It's actually one of our only potions that don't taste that bad. After you drink it you will feel some tingling in your ankle, but after you should be fine," Professor Steven says to Collin.

Collin takes the potion from the professor and begins to drink it. Just like the professor said he starts to feel the tingling in his ankle and falls onto the bed behind him. Collin chuckles a little bit as the tingling starts to tickle him.

"Is this a normal reaction?" Aria asks the professor.

"Yes, sometimes when the problem is near the feet it will begin to tickle the patient, but only until the potion kicks in. Then he should be alright," he replies.

Aria sits down by Collin and lays her head on his shoulder and holds his hand. As she started to do so, she wondered what would happen to their relationship after she finished her training. She knows deep down inside that she could possibly beat this person that is threatening her, but she starts to worry at what cost. She starts to worry that she's unnecessarily putting the people she cares about in danger. She tries to remember what her boyfriend had told her about them being aware of the risks, but was that good enough for her?

"Collin, what if I don't make it?" Aria asks.

The professor looks at her with confusion, but stays quiet and observes the conversation from a distance. Collin looks at her and puts his hand on her cheek.

"Look at me. I told you that you will. We will," Collin replies.

Aria gets frustrated and shoots up from her seat and lets out an angry sigh.

"That's not good enough Collin! I can't let you or Professor Burton do this. I have to go alone. Neither one of you can get there without me. I have to go alone. I wish you could come, but I won't risk it. If I don't come back-" Aria starts to cry.

"You will! Please don't speak like this. If you don't want us to come, we won't, but you have to promise me Aria, that you will train, and hard, before you leave us, please," Collin begs.

"I will. I have to go," Aria cries.

The professor and Collin share a look between each other.

"If that's all I can help you with I should also go. I have some things I need to take care of. Will you be alright?" Professor Steven asks.

"Yea, I'm fine," Collin reponds.

Professor Steven has also found himself growing a commitment to Aria. The more she makes herself known to the staff of the school, it seems the more they grow to care for her. Not because she doesn't have any family, not because she's a powerful witch, and not because she's stunning, but because out of all their students she is one of the most mature young ladies they have ever met. She isn't afraid to show that she cares for people, even the most hated people. She has a contagious heart. Aria could be having the worst day in her life, and somehow still brightens everyone's day around her. Professor Steven marches down to Professor Burton's classroom.

"Professor Burton, may I have a word out in the corridor?" he asks.

Professor Burton gets up and walks into the corridor silent. Following, Professor Steven grabs the chest of the other professor's shirt.

"Professor, what did you do to Miss Whitlock?" he questions.

"What are you talking about? Has it not been obvious that I've grown to care for her as my own? I suggest you get your hands off of me if you want to keep them" Professor Burton replies with pure anger.

"Why is she talking about herself dying? Not letting you and Collin go with her. What was she talking about?" Professor Steven says, blowing smoke out of his ears.

"She said that?" Professor Burton replies.

"Yes. She was talking about going somewhere, and you two not being able to get there without her. Now tell me!" Professor Steven yells.

"What the hell is going on over here. Does it look like I want my students to know all of my professors' business? I suggest you two take this up in my office or you two will not be fond of the consequences," Professor Longtail calmly interrupts.

Next thing you know the two professors along with Professor Bliss and Professor Longtial take a shameful, fast pace walk to his office. Professor Burton and Steven share glares at each other along the way. They all finally arrive in the headmasters office.

"Now, do you want to tell me what's going on?" Professor Longtail says.

"Professor Burton, I'll let you take the floor on this one," Professor Steven replies.

"Well, there's not much to say. William, you already know the details. I'm not sure why I'm being attacked," Professor Burton says sarcastically.

"Linol, what is it that's getting you so heated?" Professor Longtail asks.

"Aria has been helping me in the hospital wing. Just observing. I felt she could learn a thing or two incase she needed it. All of a sudden Collin came in and he twisted his ankle, which I fixed. She sat down next to him and started crying, thinking she was going to die and saying she had to go somewhere alone, that she no longer wanted to bring Collin nor Professor Burton," Professor Steven says.

"Linol, do you know where Aria was before she came here? Do you understand why she is not a student yet and she is just here to train?" Professor Longtail questions.

"No, why?" he replies slowly.

The three other professors all share a look of concern.

"Aria, she was imprisoned before she came here, by a wizard who had previously killed her mother. I mean, did you not see her the day she got here? Her clothes were torn, she looked exhausted, and she had no idea where she was," Professor Bliss informs.

Professor Steven expresses shock and concern.

"Why didn't any of you tell me? Do you understand how useful it would be to her to also train in the hospital? How ignorant-"

He is cut off.

"We will not talk to each other like that. If you cannot endure this conversation in a civil matter, you will not be part of it, Linol. We do not want to overwhelm her, and from what I'm hearing about her we did the right thing. She will learn in time. Unless there is a threat to our students or school, we will not rush to train Miss Whitlock. Do you understand me, professor?" William questions.

"Yes, headmaster. Are we supposed to just let her feel like this? How is she going to train at all if she's constantly distracted by the fact that mother is dead, and she might die next, let alone all the other burdens she's been facing," Professor Steven says.

"We will not let her think that. From now on, I want all three of you to spend as much time with her as you can when you see her alone. You don't have to train her every time you see her. I think we all just need to make sure she doesn't feel alone. Professor Burton, I assume this will be no problem for you," Professor Longtail says.

"No, sir" he replies.

"Now if you'd all excuse me I believe you have students to get back to," William states.

All three of the professors return to their students and continue the day like normal. Professor Longtail summons Aria to his office. He had started to do some research on the Whitlock family, and found out that her father had been sighted recently in town. He thought it'd be best for him to be as honest with her as possible.

"Hello Miss Whitlock, come in, please sit down. I summoned you here because I have some news for you about your father," Professor Longtail said.

"What? Really?" Aria questioned.

"Yes, I trust you're mature enough as to where I can be honest with you. Aria, your father was sighted in the town over recently. I didn't get very specific details, but from what I did hear, he didn't look like he planned to stay very long," he informed.

“Thanks for telling me professor, honestly I have people here that I care about and people who actually want to be in my life. I cannot force him to love me or pick me over anything else. If he does not do it on his own, that’s not my problem,” Aria replies.

“That’s very wise of you Miss Whitlock. One of your mothers friends had come to me about this. Very nice lady. I guess she’s always known that your family were wizards. She captured a photo, would you like to see?” the professor asked.

“I think so?” she replies.

Professor Longtail hands Aria the photo and she stares at it confused. Not to mention his robe looked familiar but she couldn’t figure out from where.

“Everything alright?” the professor questioned.

“What’s this thing behind him? She asked.

She hands the photo to the professor and points to the corner of the photo. There appears to be some sort of red orb, part of it anyways.

“Can I keep this photo professor?” Aria asks.

“Of course, by all means. Just be careful, please,” he pleads.

Aria takes the photo and rushes herself to find Collin. She finds him in the common room, one of them anyway.

“Collin! I need you to come with me to the library, please come,” Aria asks.

"I would, but I have one more class right now, after that I'm available the rest of the night. Would you like to meet there in an hour?" Collin asks.

"Um, sure. I'm going to go right now and get a head start, if I'm not there when you're done you can probably find me with Professor Burton," she replies.

Collin nods and continues to walk to his class. Aria doesn't think she knows the library well enough to go seek for the information herself so she goes to seek Professor Burton. Conveniently, he didn't have a class. She knocked on the door and saw him face deep in a textbook.

"Hi, it's just me, what's that you're reading?" Aria questions.

"Well this happens to be a book about speed traveling. I'm reading about how it has to be passed down from a parent. Only about four to seven wizard families on the planet have the ability to speed travel," Professor Burton states.

"That's amazing. I came here to ask a favor of you, if you have some time. I spoke with the headmaster and one of my mothers friends had seen my father in the town over. She captured a photo of him, but there is something in the background that I need to figure out what it is, will you help me?" she asks.

Aria wasn't sure if she had said something wrong but the professor's face had suddenly shifted once she mentioned her father.

"I can definitely help you with this Miss Whitlock," he replies.

They walk to the big red door, and she notices the professor opens the door with his wand, and she wonders why Collin didn't open it the same way. They sit down at the table to investigate the photo. Professor Burton understands that it looks like some kind of portal. He pulls out his wand once again and casts a spell that allows him to summon the books including the topic that he needs. He starts to speed read through the books and Aria was quite surprised because she thought she was going to help.

"Here. It's a portal that allows one to travel through other dimensions. One would use this portal if he or she did not possess the gift of speed traveling. It can be created by a simple spell, but only spoken from a powerful wizard," the professor says.

Aria snatches the photo from the table.

"I can't believe it. Why would he do this? To me, to our family, I don't understand," Aria cries.

"What are you talking about?" asked the professor.

"That must be why his robe looked so familiar when I first saw the photo. You have to be kidding. I can't handle this. I can't do this," she says.

"Aria, tell me," Professor Burton demands.

"My father, he killed my mother, and he's the one who took me to the prison, but why? I don't understand any of this. This is very overwhelming. I need to go," Aria pleads.

Aria then runs out of the library and finds her room. As she starts to shed a tear she notices her mothers photo. She sensed a bad feeling about it. Something was off. Aria grabs the photo of her mother and takes it to Professor Longtail. Unfortunately for her, he was busy. She then seeks any professor she can find, with the photo in her pocket.

"Professor Bliss, wait a minute please. Do you have a moment to speak alone," Aria said.

They walked together to the common room, all the other children were in class.

"What do you need dear?" Professor Bliss replies.

"I need you to see if there's any dark magic in this photo. I would do it, but I'm not sure how. I haven't learned that far just yet," Aria asks.

"Well alright, give it here," says the professor.

She takes the photo and raises her wand.

"Zoronum," she says.

"What's that do?" Aria asked.

"This is a spell you cast upon an object which possesses dark magic. It will not tell you who did it, or what they did, but will give you an obvious clue. It makes you figure it out. It will change the object," says the professor.

The photo began to float and change shape. It had appeared to change into a camera. Aria first thought it didn't work because it was a photo, taken with a camera.

"Do you know what this means?" the professor asked.

"No, unfortunately," Aria says.

"Aria dear, if it turned into a camera, it means someone wanted to watch you," Professor Bliss states.

"Like spy on me? Why me?" Aria wonders.

"Sometimes it gets difficult to release dark magic from an object. Do you mind if I keep it for a little while?" Professor Bliss questioned.

"That's fine. Honestly you can keep it for now. I think I know who did this and it's best if he doesn't have access to me," Aria replied.

Professor Bliss took the photo. Aria goes back to Professor Burton's classroom. She felt bad for the way she left, she felt she may have hurt his feelings. The whole time it takes her to get to his room, she wonders how she is going to tell Professor Burton that her father is still alive, not only alive, but also he's the one coming for her. She finally arrives at his room.

"Professor?" she calls.

"Yes, I'm here. What's going on?" Professor Burton asks.

"I need you to sit down and listen to me. I talk, you listen. Please?" Aria begged.

"Alright?" he replies.

"Alright, well I wanna start by saying I apologize for the way I left. Considering the trust you put in me I felt awful after I did that. Secondly, that photo is my father. That photo is also a picture of the man who murdered my mother and imprisoned me. I remember his robe from the night my mother passed away. All three of the men were wearing the same robe. I just don't understand why he would hurt us. Last, but not least, when I first came here I brought a photo of my mother. One day it had disappeared and today it was there again. I got a bad feeling and took it to Professor Bliss. Turns out someone was spying on me through the photo. They used dark magic. This is really scary for me, professor. I'm scared my father will kill me as well," Aria explained.

"I'm really sorry to hear that. It must not be easy. If it's not too soon to ask, what was your mothers name?" Professor Burton questions.

"Her name was Sarah. She passed just a couple nights weeks before I came here. She was so loving. I never felt loved by my father. He just had such evil intent his whole life and seemed to hate me and my mother but I don't know why," she replied.

"Your mothers name was Sarah Whitlock? What color was her hair or eyes if you don't mind?" the professor questioned.

It's okay I like to talk about her. She was very different. Her hair was made up of beautiful honey brown locks, and her eyes were dark brown like mine, but she had special eyes. I don't think I have ever seen eyes like hers," Aria explains.

As Aria explains the details of her mother she says one thing in particular that the professor was hoping not to hear.

"You see, her eyes had green in them, but only toward the inside of her eyes. So on her right eye, it was green on the left side, and on the left eye, it was green on the right. I bet that confuses you, but I'm not sure how else to explain it," Aria says.

Professor Burton stares at Aria as she explains with a feared look on his face. All the thoughts that were running through his head couldn't be read by anyone. She starts to notice his very specific attention to detail.

"Are you okay, professor?" she asks.

"Have you happened to see Professor Longtail anywhere?" he asks.

"I went to his office before I asked Professor Bliss to manage the photo, but he wasn't there. I'm not sure if he's back yet or not. Are you alright?" she questions.

"Yes, but I must go. I will find you later," Professor Burton concludes.

Aria thought he started acting weird during the time she was describing her mother.

"Wait professor," Aria said.

"What is it?" he asked in a hurry.

"How do you know my mother?" she questions.

Professor Burton freezes. He wasn't sure what to say. He didn't want to lie to Aria, but he also felt this wasn't the right time to tell her.

"Aria, you're right. I did know your mother, but I can't tell you how. Not now. There will come a time I feel you are ready but the time right now isn't good for that. Focus on what you need to do and someday we will talk about it. I promise," Professor Burton replied.

"Okay, but if you lie to me, or take advantage of me in any way professor, I will not take it lightly. I want to believe you will not underestimate me," Aria concludes.

Aria confidently walked out of his classroom trying not to break her cover. After she left his room she took a breath of relief. She wasn't sure where that aggression came from. She thought to herself it may just be a natural defense mechanism.

Aria decided to go to the library and see if there was anything there that she could possibly teach herself.

She walked kindly to the library, and as she sat down she took a moment. She really needed it. There is a lot of pressure on her shoulders and sometimes it can be stressful. Sometimes she felt like everything was moving way too fast for her, and then other times things weren't moving fast enough. One day she feels loved by her peers, and then the next day she feels like she's flying solo. She feels alone. Something about Aria is she craves adventure, she loves to be the best at what she does including the praise she gets. It makes her feel less alone, but part of her likes the private and homely feeling. It's not easy to have to balance inbetween for some people and Aria just so happens to be one of them.

Aria goes to find a book, any book would do. She sits in the library for hours watching the people come and go as they please. She notices the freedom and the trust the professors possess within their students. She wonders if they trust her the same way. I mean they must, she was a stranger in the beginning and they were so giving to her. Aria continues to read book after book just letting the time pass. As she was doing so she began to hear a noise.

"Hello? Is someone there?" she pleads.

She gets up to investigate the noise but continues to find absolutely nothing. At this point she doesn't even know if she's scared or confused, or both. She walks around the corner of one of the book shelves and she notices an envelope thrown at the ground. It says her name. She slowly picks it up and looks around to see if there is anyone there with her, but there is not. Opening the letter to find the words,

"Come to me, join me, serve me. Or DIE!".

"What the hell is this, a game? This has to be from the man who killed my mother," she quietly says to herself.

Aria wasn't sure if she wanted to show this letter to the headmaster. She didn't want the school to think she was putting them in danger, but it also might be the right thing to do. She takes the envelope and decides to bring it to Professor Burton. She walked to his classroom but he was not there. He happened to be with the headmaster. She continued to look around the school for the professor.

"Please William, you have to believe me. What other explanation would you have for this? What if I was able to provide you with her hair or saliva, could you test it?" Professor Burton says.

"I suppose if you managed to get your hands on a single strand of her hair, I would be able to test it. You cannot let her know about this, not until it is proven that she is your daughter," Professor Longtail replies.

"Of course, professor. When do you need it?" Professor Burton replies.

"I need it by tonight. I will look up a recipe as should you, as you are the concoctions professor," Professor Longtail answers.

"I'll try to see what I can find, sir," Professor Burton says.

Professor Burton starts to head to his classroom, but he happens to see Aria, but this time she has kind of a shaken, or frozen look on her face. He wasn't sure what it was about. He sees the envelope in her hand and asks her what it's for.

"Hello professor. I really should get going, I have something I need to take care of," Aria says, knowing he will ask what's in her hand.

"What's this for?" he asks.

"Oh um, well I was just minding my business in the library and I heard something. I looked around but there was no one there with me. Then I saw this on the floor around one of the book shelves. I'm starting to get really worried. This isn't normal," Aria informs the professor.

The professor takes the envelope and reads it. He has a gastly look on his face. He wants to tell Aria so badly that she might be his daughter, but he didn't want to bring it up if he was wrong.

"Aria, who's this from?" he asks.

"I don't know, probably whoever you're training me for, professor," she says.

"Look at me, we'll figure it out together. I will never let anything happen to you Aria, trust me. Please," the professor proceeds sentimentally.

Aria goes in to hug the professor and before she pulls away the professor notices a loose strand of her hair sitting on the shoulder on her school robe. He carefully pulls it. He's never done anything so subtle before. At this point he hopes she is his daughter so he's not taking her hair for no reason. Aria releases him and tells him she needs to take care of something. He makes sure he doesn't drop the hair and waits for her to walk away before he leaves in a hurry. He speeds right back to the headmasters office.

"Welcome Professor Burton, back for more already?" Professor Longtail says.

"Yes, well no sir. I have a strand of her hair. She was actually on her way here I presume. Here, take this. I think you should read it. Aria claims to have found this in the library while she was alone. I'm not sure what this means exactly but I don't think this person has good intentions," Professor Burton says.

"Yes, I see that. I will bring her in here after we're done brewing her strand of hair. I assume you'd like to get that done first?" William asks.

"Of course, I'll start that immediately," he replies.

Aria starts to overthink about the letter she found. She doesn't want to be putting anyone in danger on behalf of herself. She knows that the more she learns about herself, she will be one of the top witches of the world, but at what cost she wonders. The only person she thinks of turning to at a time like this is Colin. Professor Burton would freak out, and Professor Longtail would try to take matters in his own hands. So Aria decides to find Collin training in one of the courtyards. He's teaching the first years how to manage their brooms, and keep from getting splinters.

"Hi, would you have a minute to talk? I have some news, and I wanted to tell you first," Aria says.

"Yes, what's going on?" Collin asks.

"I got a really bad letter today. I'm not sure who it's from but I'm pretty sure it's from whomever murdered my mom. I think I'm going to leave from here next week. I'll have to find somewhere else private enough to train until I'm ready. I'm so sorry, and I'll really miss you," Aria says as she sheds a tear for Collin.

"What? No. I know there's something we can do, please Aria," Collin begs.

"Please don't make this harder than it already is. I can't even say goodbye to the professors because they will not want me to leave. They've been so good to me as well, I can't bear to say goodbye. I'll miss them so much, but I guess fighting with a broken heart makes you stronger. This doesn't mean we have to break up Collin," Aria replies.

"That's not the point, I don't want you to leave. We're only sixteen Aria, you could spend two more years here. With me, learning fun and creative spells. Isn't that something you desire?" Collin asks.

"Oh hun, I wish it was that easy. He wants me so badly, he won't stop until he gets what he wants or unless I stop him before that happens. I'm a very talented witch and I know that I have a lot to learn, but I need your trust Collin. My loved ones trust is my motivation to keep going, I just want to say that if I don't come back, I love you. I know it's early, but like I said I'm talented and I know what I want," she says.

Collin gives her a look of despair, and continues to tend to his students once again. Aria wants to tell Professor Burton about this but she is scared he will hate her. He's had a history of distancing and detachment and Aria can't figure out if she's special enough to him where he won't distance from her. Collin on the other hand was confident enough to go to Professor Burton, mostly because Collin was not emotionally invested and he knew the professor could convince Aria to stay. Collin finishes up with his students a little while later and starts heading for Professor Burton. He finally gets to his classroom.

"Professor Burton? Are you here?" he says aloud.

"Yes I am. What can I do for you Collin, how are your studies going?" Professor Burton questions.

The professor has never asked Collin this before, perhaps it is because he is committed to Aria.

"Well we need to talk. I'm going to need you to sit down and listen to me. Aria wants to leave the school. She thinks she is endangering us and the other students. She doesn't want to tell any of the staff because she thinks you'll try to stop her. She can't leave, professor. I love her, and if she leaves I will too. I will follow her and make sure she is safe," Collin pleads.

"First of all if you want to be kicked out I suppose you could leave, but if not I suggest you plant your feet and let us handle this. When did you find this out?" the professor asks, as his heart sinks to his feet completely broken.

"She came and found me in the courtyard while I was mentoring the first years. Professor she seems to really connect with you, more than me even. I need you to convince her to stay. She's so delicate with everything going on you can't just be straightforward with her or she'll leave and never come back," Collin informs.

"I will try to figure this out, in the meantime I suggest you distance a little bit, you piss her off one time and she'll be gone quicker than you can mount your broom," says the professor.

Collin acknowledges the professor's wish and continues with his day. It wasn't the fact that Aria had special gifts, or that in the near future she may be one of the best witches on earth, but Collin just feels so drawn to Aria whenever she's around. She makes his day, she is Collin's motivation. He doesn't even understand how he could love someone so soon after meeting them. That only happens in movies and in books he thinks to himself. Although he knew it would be really difficult to distance from her, he did his best. There is a field nearby the school and Collin goes there. Once Collin is finally at the field, he pulls out his wand. Not saying anything he starts to zap everything around him. He cries with anger. It feels as if Aria has died, in his heart. He hasn't ever felt pain like this before, and how to handle it he is unsure of. He screams so loud that everyone at the border, or even with a window open at the school could hear him, Professor Burton being one of them.

Collin starts to head back to the school, but as he does so he feels like he is being followed. Taken over by his emotions, he doesn't care if he was or not. Suddenly a cloke is placed on top of his head, he is filled with regret as soon as the light turns into darkness, and he is put in a choke hold until he passes out. Later on he finally wakes up, in a place of concrete and chain. Fortunately he knew exactly where he was. Unfortunately there was nothing he could do. The men had broken his wand in half. When a man comes in to give him some food and water, Collin decides to speak.

"Hey! Good luck, she's not even at the school anymore. I'm warning you, you will not win," Collin says, out of breath from struggling.

The other man in the room walks off in silence.

"You're a damn coward!" Collin screams.

The door shuts behind the guard and Collin is left with nothing but silence. He realizes what consistent silence can do to a person. There were good things and bad things. You could truly start to look inside yourself and discover things about yourself that you didn't even think existed. On the other hand, for some the silence will drive them insane. They won't know what to do with themselves, it's something that we can naturally control so when that ability is taken from us, it consumes us and they lose track of who they are.

Professor Burton takes this new found information to the headmaster hoping he doesn't already know. He struts to Professor Bliss's classroom as she is the nearest professor to him. He kindly asks her if she has seen the headmaster, but she has not. Professor Burton heads to the headmasters office and there he is, sitting on a chair that looks like a throne, and reading the pages of a massive old book.

"Excuse me, William. I'm afraid we have a problem. I wasn't so sure if you were already aware?" Professor Burton hints.

"What is it, are the students alright?" Professor Longtail questions.

"Yes, the students are alright, but headmaster it's about Aria. She wants to leave. She's worried about putting Collin or I in danger, but I don't believe she is ready to fight on her own," he replies.

"I see, but we can not stop her. If she wishes to go, we have to let her go. This is not a prison, but a school we definitely are. The only thing we can do is teach her. The most important thing is that she remembers to ask for help when it is well needed. She thinks she can do everything on her own, but Professor Burton I'm afraid that is not how the world works," Professor Longtail lectures.

"Professor, there has been something that I've been meaning to discuss with you. I know I might be pushing it, But have you happened to have a chance to test her hair? We need proof," Professor Burton said.

"What's the story with you and her mother anyways?" William replied.

"I knew her mother when we were younger. It was before Aria was even born. I loved her mother, but she was committed to someone else. Time happened, and they decided to get married, but the night before the wedding Sarah came to see me. She wanted to have one night, just for us. We talked, we danced, we talked more. One thing led to another and we made love. Nine months later Aria was born, but I had to stay away because I promised her mother I would. I never knew if she was mine or not, until she came here. She's a speed traveler, William. As am I," he replied.

"Does her mother, or her father possess this ability?" Professor Longtail questions.

"No, I asked her when she showed me, she said they couldn't. That's why I was so shocked when she showed me because as you know speed traveling has to be passed down," Professor Burton worries.

"Did you finish brewing the potion?" Professor Longtail asks.

"Yes," he replies.

"Dump it in this. If the water turns green she is yours, if it turns blue, she is not. It should only take a few seconds," Professor Longtail informs.

Professor Burton pours his brew into a big and beautiful bowl of glowing water. As the pigments of the water start to change both professors stand still with anticipation in their hearts. The water continues to wiggle, but won't change from the clear silver color in which the water originated. The two share a look, and when they look back the water is green. Grabbing onto his heart, Professor Burton collapses to the floor spitting out nothing short of a silent cry.

"I'm so sorry," Professor Longtail says sympathetically.

"I've missed all these years of her life, William. I don't know what I'm going to say to her," Professor Burton cries.

"I'm sure Aria would appreciate the truth. Maybe you could talk to her before she leaves," William states.

Professor Burton, filled with so many emotions, had sped to his classroom. Very unsure of what to do, he comes to the conclusion that he will not tell Aria. Not yet, anyways. Professor Burton had realized he had a few more training sessions with Aria left so he went to find her to let her know to meet him in the courtyard that afternoon. He can tell that Aria is very stressed and is starting to lose her focus.

"Is there something troubling you Aria?" Professor Burton asks.

"Yes actually, I talked to Collin earlier about some rather personal things, and I haven't seen him anywhere. I'm worried something bad happened to him. It's hard for me to focus not knowing where he is," Aria replied.

"I'm sure he is around the school somewhere, after all this is a very big school," Professor Burton reassures.

"You don't understand. What we talked about really bothered him. I can feel it, something is wrong. I'm sorry professor but I need to go, I'll see you later for training," Aria leaves.

Professor Burton watches Aria walk away in distress. He wants to tell her so badly, but how could he? With all the stuff she's currently going through, he would just make things worse for her. He hopes that she will keep her word and show up to training because something is telling him that she might not.

The day goes by pretty quickly for everyone. It seems as if something in the school has changed. Not only with Aria and Collin and the professors, but with all the students as well. Such a negative energy. Some of the students' grades even start to drop and this is becoming alarming to Professor Bliss because she's the only one that seems to notice these changes. She decides to take it up with the headmaster hoping that he will know what to do.

"So what should we do? This isn't normal. This has never happened to our school before. We need to fix it," Professor Bliss says.

"I was afraid these times would come. Something big will happen. I'm not sure when, or if we will even see it, but it is coming. I think we should gather all the students and have a feast. It may take their minds off of whatever is going on. Including Aria and Collin and of course Professor Burton," the headmaster says.

"Alright, I shall make an announcement. I really hope this works," Professor Bliss praises.

Professor Bliss makes the announcement to the whole school, come the following meal.

"Alright everyone listen up. In light of recent events we have decided to throw a feast. It will take place next week during dinner on Friday," she announces.

While she is happy with the announcement, the students don't look very pleased. Perhaps a feast will not change anything. The headmaster also notices this.

"And all exams for next week have been canceled," she says as she takes her seat.

All the professors looked shocked, wondering if that had come from the headmaster or from her, meanwhile the headmaster winked at Professor Bliss, allowing her to relax and realize she's not in trouble for saying that. The students started to cheer. It feels for everyone as if whatever weight has been placed, has lifted a bit. Everyone continues to eat their food and chat, except for one person. Where could she be? Has she left so soon? Professor Burton leans over to Professor Bliss.

"Could you assist me with something?" he asks.

"What might that be?" she replies.

"Well I haven't seen Aria, I was wondering if you could look for her and bring her here to eat. She hasn't been eating and I think it may be better for her if another woman speaks with her. Please?" he begs.

"Of course. I'll be right back." she says.

Professor bliss then gets up unannounced and starts walking towards the end of the dining room. She peaks the corner and there happens to be Aria, unfortunately she was sitting there in pain. She was crying, very hard.

Professor Bliss slowly walks over to Aria and sits down next to her. Not saying anything, Aria notices and leans over into Professor Bliss's arms. At a shock Professor Bliss wraps her arms around her, knowing that once in a while all we need to do is cry.

"Let it out, Aria," Professor Bliss says.

"I'm scared. Collin is missing. Did he do this because of me? Because I'm leaving next week? Or did something bad happen to him? I don't understand. This wasn't supposed to be this hard professor. Collin doesn't know this, but my mother had come to me in my dream the first time I met him. She said I would spend a lifetime with him. She also said to trust Professor Burton but I'm not sure what that was about. If I'm supposed to spend a lifetime with Collin, why did he run away?" Aria cried

"He's probably in the dining room, we can go look together okay?" Professor Bliss suggested.

The two go into the dining area and look for Collin but he seems not to be there. This just makes Aria feel even worse. Standing by the doors of the dining room Aria remains to cry as Professor Bliss remains to hold her. Professor Burton notices this all the way from the other end of the dining hall. He gets very worried, but is afraid to show it. His curiosity burns him with passion, but he'd still rather have Aria's mind be safe from what he knows. Professor Bliss takes Aria out of the dining hall and continues out into the corridor. It hurts Professor Burton because in wizard families of such power that he and Aria possess, their hearts are connected. So when she feels this way he doesn't even have to be around her to know it. Dinner has finally come to an end and it's time for Aria to meet Professor Burton in the courtyard for another training session.

"Hey Professor Burton, do you think we could do this another time, I'm not sure if I'm up for it today." Aria says.

"No," he replied.

"No? Why not?" Aria asks.

"Well if you plan to leave next week you'll need all the training you can get. Suck it up and let us begin," he replies.

"Wait a minute, how do you know about that?" she asks.

"Well your boyfriend came to me after you told him, hoping that I would stop you from leaving, and as much as I want to do so I am not allowed to. The only thing I can do is teach you as much as I can until you're gone, and you need to remember to ask for help when it is needed," Professor Burton says.

"Does that mean you know where he is?" she asks.

"Who might you be talking about?" he replies.

"Collin of course. Clearly you were the last to speak to him. He is missing professor. That's why I've been having such a hard day," she replies.

"I did not know he was gone, no I'm not sure where he went but I'm sure he'll come back. Aria he seems to really love you. A little distance in love doesn't mean they're gone forever. I promise you will see him again, okay?" Professor Burton states.

"Well alright, let's just get this over with please," she says.

"Okay, wand at the ready. Now I want you to point your wand at the lock in front of you and say 'Entra Lotose', okay?" he informs.

"Entra Lotose," she says.

The lock bursts open.

"I want you to know this will not work on every single lock you try it on, but most. It will be more than helpful when you go to your father," Professor Burton says.

"Yes, my father of course. I just can't believe he would do such a thing. He wasn't a good person, professor but this is extreme even for him. He would treat me and my mother very poorly. We would have so much fun especially with magic, when he wasn't around. I fear my mother was scared of him, but I refuse to go down that same path," Aria says.

"I trust you and I believe you Aria, you're strong and I'm on your side, always. Now get up and let's keep practicing. This is a spell in which you can levitate and control an object or even a person and make them do whatever you want them to. Point your wand at me, and say 'Incartum Levanais'. Try it," he informs.

"Incartum Levanais," she says.

Professor Burton was curious about what she would do to him. She made him levitate into the air. Then she made him twirl a few times. Finally she sped him over to her, right in front of her, and she set him down. She gave him a loving hug, and stepped back.

"Well I think we could fit in one more. This is a powerful offensive spell. This will definitely help you with your father. Point your wand at that shrub, and say 'Delictum'." he says.

"Delictum!" she says.

The shrub explodes right before her eyes. Aria has never used magic as such, seeing as though she has never had to fight. She was amazed with the things she started to learn about herself. The things she could do. She started to think about all the people around her that couldn't do half of what she could and she started to be even more grateful for what she possesses. Most people would kill for a gift like hers. She is thankful that she is someone who uses her powers for good, unlike some.

"Professor, can I ask you something?" Aria asks.

"Of course you can," he replies.

"Why is it that certain wizards go bad? I don't mean that they just wanted more power than everyone else, but something must happen to them where they are not happy. When I was younger I thought my father was happy with me and my mother and now my whole life just seems like time wasted," Aria says.

"Well sometimes there are things that we just aren't able to understand. A lot of wizards who go dark usually tend to keep their private life a secret. It could be used as a weapon against them, or they just don't want people to know. Usually us on the better side of wizardry don't like to pry," Professor Burton replies.

"Well thank you, and thanks for today. It kind of made me feel better in a way. I just wanna say I really appreciate you being here and always having my back and being there at the worst moments of mine. Maybe you should have been my father," she chuckled.

Professor Burton smiles and tells her to go to bed. The more time that goes by the worse he wants to tell Aria that she is his daughter. Aria goes back to her room once again. She doesn't even know what to think about her day or the days to come. It's hard for her to just take it one day at a time because she had so much to think about. She gets into her bed and has trouble falling asleep. The biggest burden on her mind happened to be Collin. She couldn't do anything but think the worst.

"Until tomorrow," she whispers, as she gently falls asleep.

She starts to dream of herself in a beautiful field of flowers, laying her head down, looking at the deep blue sky. It feels as if she may be in heaven. Then the sky turned red, and it started storming right before her eyes. All of a sudden she sees a man at the other end of the huge field starting to slowly walk up to her. It seems as if he's taken so long to reach her. Aria realizes it's her father. She wonders what he wants and if this could actually be real.

"Come to me Aria, for you will not be happy if I have to come to you at that precious school of yours. My darling daughter, what a fool you are to think this would be the last of us. How is your friend Collin by the way? It is my understanding that you don't know where he is?" Oliver Whitlock states.

"What did you do to him? Why are you doing this? I thought you loved me and mom. I know you murdered her. I don't understand why. Please tell me?" Aria asks.

"Yes, your mother. Never pleased, never satisfied. Your mother was very selfish. She took what was mine and gave it to another, but I assume you already know that," he replies slowly.

"What are you talking about? Whatever it is I'm sure it's not enough of a reason to become who you've become," Aria states.

"So you don't know?" he asks while laughing in her face.

"I don't know what?" she demands

"Before you were born your mother was disloyal to me. I never forgave her, but be warned that is not what shaped me into who I am today," he says.

"Then what did?" she asked.

"Power. It is something that not many have. There are so many amazing things that you can do with power. You see darling, you have some very amazing gifts. Ones that neither me nor your mother had ever had. In which you are not my child," he says.

Aria wakes up in a panic, and looks out the window to see the sun shining. She doesn't know who to go to, but she feels the need to talk to someone about this. Breakfast finally starts and everyone is in the dining hall. Having no friends Aria slowly walks up to the big table at the front where the professors sit, and the whole school has become silent. It is clear to her that a rare amount of students do this.

"Professor Burton, may I sit here? I don't have any friends and I don't know anyone here. I'm not comfortable sitting down there," she pleads.

"Of course, you can sit next to me on one condition," he replies.

"What's that?" Aria asks.

"Please, eat something," he demands.

Aria shook her head in acceptance. Everyone in the room was filled with shock that she had asked the one professor who probably would have said no to anyone else. The students had wondered what was so different about her. How she connected with the staff better than the ones her own age.

"Professor, can we speak about something?" she asks.

"Sure," he replies.

“Last night something happened, with my father. He came to me in my dream, he,” she pauses.

“What? What is it?” Professor Burton demands. His heart pounding, hands sweaty.

“He has Collin. I couldn’t bear to see Collin dead. He said something really weird to me and I don’t know how to feel about it or if it was true, I mean he really has no reason to lie. He told me my mother had cheated on him before I was born. That I have powers that none of my parents had, that I wasn’t his child,” she cries, not knowing all the staff just heard what she said.

Professor Burton freezes and looks over to the headmaster, the headmaster nods his head at the professor. Professor Burton puts his arm around Aria, continuing to keep his secret until the right time. He stays silent. After a few seconds she finishes her food and heads to see Professor Steven.

Aria knocks on the door, but he is not there. She walks in anyways. Following her, a student who has had an accident resulting in a broken hand.

“Hi, my name is Rosalie. Do you know where Professor Steven is? I think I broke my hand. It hurts really bad,” Rosalie says.

“No I’m sorry, is there something I can do?” Aria replies.

“If you know how to fix a broken hand that would be amazing,” the girl replied, as she screamed in pain.

Because of Rosalie and her screams the other staff start heading to the hospital wing.

"Oh my gosh, okay um, let me try something," Aria says.

Aria pulls the girl's hand out from beneath her robe and places one of her hands on top and the other on the bottom of the other girl's hand. Aria gently closes her eyes and invisions all the bones being put into the right place with a more healing energy. A bright blue light starts to appear from their hands, and Rosalie can literally feel the broken bones starting to mend their bond once again. Professor Longtail, Bliss, and Burton all stand there awaiting Aria to finish. Flabbergasted by something in which they have never seen before.

"How mysterious," Professor Longtail intriguingly whispers to the other professors.

"Indeed," Professor Bliss replies with a huge smile on her face.

Professor Burton on the other hand was not surprised at all. He knew Aria was capable of amazing things and it was only in a matter of time that she'd start showing them. He was extremely proud of her. What she was becoming right before his eyes. In some way, it started to make up for the years he missed. Professor Burton has always come to terms with the fact that with good, will also come bad, and with bad, will also come good. Professor Burton tried to believe that time never existed, it was just an illusion brought upon the mortal world, but if they are so fooled by time, how does he make sure his world is not?

Aria proceeds to open her eyes. The first thing she sees is Rosalie smiling from ear to ear. The next thing she notices are all the professors staring at her in such a fascinated manner. She looks at the girl's hand to find it better than it was before it was broken.

"Professor Longtail, I didn't know I could even do that," Aria stuttered with a proud smile.

"Will you come with me to my office along with the other professors please?" Professor Longtail asks.

They took a joyful walk through the school to get to the headmasters office. Aria was wondering what they were going to say and if it would be good or not so much.

They finally get to the office and the headmaster stands next to his chair as Aria stands before him on the other side of his massive desk.

"Aria I brought you in here today because I want to stress the importance of your practices. Following the battle with your father, if you wish to come back, I would like for you to be an official student here at our academy. You have the potential to be one of the greatest witches of your time, and you have shown that potential on many occasions. I am very proud, but very curious of how far deep into your powers we can discover over time," Professor Longtail says.

"Professor I would absolutely love to be here for as long as I could but I don't think I have the money for a place like this. If I can't afford it I want all of you guys to know how much I have appreciated your guidance. I wouldn't be able to do any of this without you, especially you Professor Burton, thanks," Aria replies.

"Dear, we don't need your money, you already have a school robe and a wand, the only thing that would be left is books and I think I have some things you could do to earn a little money. Can I just ask, what's your dream profession if I may?" he replies.

"I'm not sure to be quite honest. I've told you before that I have always known I was a witch. I kind of like the idea of being able to help others, not even just physically, but teaching others how to use their magic and find magic within themselves that they never knew they had," Aria replies.

"So, one could say a professor of some sort?" Professor Longtail questions

"I guess so, yeah," Aria confirms.

The headmaster nodded his head. He then informed the other professors that he needed to get some work done. He advised Aria and Professor Burton to stay back a moment.

"Miss Whitlock I just felt the need to ask where you will be staying if you don't feel like you can come back here?" Professor Longtail questioned.

"I guess I haven't planned for much after I go see my father. I'm not even sure if I will win. He is a powerful man," Aria said.

Something then clicked in Aria's brain in front of both Professor Burton and the headmaster.

"Professor Longtail, besides dreams, do you know if there is any other way that I can contact my father prior to going and seeing him? I want to know why it was so easy for me to, well I better keep that between him and I for now, but would you happen to know of anything?" Aria asks.

Professor Burton felt kind of hurt that she did not want to share this with him, but after all he has secrets of his own.

"There are not many options. I suggest you try to find the answers you're looking for elsewhere before you do something that you could possibly regret," he replies.

"Would there be anything about communication between different dimensions in the library here at the school?" Aria asks.

"I don't know you'll have to go look when you have some time. I do not by any means want to put you two on the spot, but knowing that Miss Whitlock hasn't been thinking for herself, maybe she could live with you off campus Professor Burton? Or if you would like to come back to school you can stay here until you're eight-teen, and then live with Professor Burton. Would you like that?" Professor Longtail asks.

"Of course. I bet his house has black drapes and a black couch and black bedding," Aria and the headmaster chuckle.

"Professor Burton, would you be alright with this?" the headmaster says.

"Of course," he smiles at Aria.

Aria had started doing amazing things for the other students. She figured it would make up for her not really talking to anyone the whole time she's been there. She would fix broken books, magical objects including wands, she could even heal a broken heart if she concentrated really hard, with no interruptions of course. Not only the professors started to notice how amazing Aria was, but also the students. They would talk about all the stuff she did for them no matter how big or small. The word eventually got around, and Aria started to think people were talking poorly about her. It was quite the opposite. She headed down to Professor Burton's room.

"Professor, hi how are you?" she asks.

"I'm doing alright, yourself?" he replies.

"Well, I have something that's been bothering me but I don't know how to talk about it without sounding like, well a loser," she chuckled saldy.

"What's going on, and you're not a loser okay?" he said caringly.

"Well I have been trying really hard to make some friends or even just to be nice to people. Fixing things for them, getting them out of trouble, and even helping in the hospital wing, but no one has tried to be my friend. They just look at me and start talking. I'm worried that it's because Collin is missing and it's my fault," Aria cried.

"Aria Collin will turn up again. I promise. As for the other students, as much as I hate to say it, you're not here to make friends. I believe you should worry about that later when everything settles down. Lunch is approaching. I suggest you start heading over there. You may sit with the professors," he stated.

Aria walked to the dining room. It started to feel like home in the castle. Having Professor Burton was like having a dad. Having Professor Bliss was like having a step-mother, and not the evil kind. Having Professor Longtail was like having a wise grandfather, and Professor Steven like an uncle. Aria was really starting to appreciate the staff, more than the students. She felt like she had a family again, and before coming here she was an only child and other had her mother and father, so an even bigger family.

In light of everything going on, Aria had become more comfortable with her place in the school. She felt she belonged, and also deserved respect, but she also remembered she is still a kid. She wants to make friends more than anything. She wanted friends that once they were older, it didn't mean the end of their friendship. She wanted life long relationships, and in the world of magic that is usually how friends work. Everyone finally started to arrive for lunch, taking their seats and chatting with their cliques. Aria of course at the professor's table. She decided to stand up and stand in front of the table, and get everyone's attention. The professor's were extremely curious as to what would happen next.

"Hello everyone. My name is Aria and I would like your attention for just a minute. I want you guys to know that I have been trying really hard to be as nice as I can to everyone here. All of you guys. It's been really hard for me to make friends. I have a feeling it may be because the only friend I had is now missing. I feel you guys deserve the truth. My father took Collin to try to get to me. He is a really bad man. The reason I am not in classes with you guys is because I'm training really hard just to have to go and kill my own father. It's a lot easier said than done. He was never a good dad, but that doesn't mean he wasn't there my entire life. For those of you that aren't very fond of me I have good news, and bad news. The good news is that I'm leaving next week to go to battle if you wish to call it that. The bad news is that if I survive, I'm coming here to finish the two last years I have here. I miss Collin, well I miss my boyfriend so terribly. This is really hard for me. I just want to ask, maybe cut me some slack, thank you." Aria announces.

All the students mesmerized by Aria's speech continued to eat and chat, as well as the professors.

Professor Burton was a little worried. It seems it may be difficult for Aria to kill her "father", and if her father takes advantage of that Aria won't even last a second and Professor Burton was well aware of this. He decided to put it in their next lesson together. Aria looked kind of down throughout the rest of lunch until a girl and her brother decided to come up to the professors table and show some appreciation.

"I'm sorry professors, but me and my brother wanted to introduce ourselves. I am Ryan, and my brother's name is Reginald but everyone calls him Reggie. You're welcome to sit by us whenever. We kindly stay to ourselves. We just wanted to know that no one here thinks poorly of you. Everyone praises you, but they're afraid to be your friend because we all see you're really powerful and sometimes when a witch hasn't had real training her powers can do whatever they want. We just didn't want to get hurt but you seem to have control over yourself. I'm really proud of how you're handling things. We have to go but talk later!" Ryan introduces.

This made Aria's day so much better. She never thought someone would go up to the professors table just to talk to her. Aria couldn't stop thinking about it for the rest of the day.

It seemed like no matter how many times Aria had a burst of encouragement, her self doubt would pummel all her confidence. She would wonder if she was good enough, or if she was smart enough. All it took for her to continue and not be fearful was one person standing in her corner. Then again, sometimes it seemed no matter how many people were in that corner, she was alone. Aria's mind had never worked like anyone else's, it was just a matter of time before she learned how to use it to her benefit. There was no inbetween for Aria, either love and light or darkness and evil. She sees the mortal and magic world in such detail.

Professor Burton couldn't stop playing a vision in his head of Aria's supposid father getting in Aria's head during the fight, and Aria losing. I believe I mentioned Professor Burton is one of the most powerful wizards of them all. He decided to go down into the basement of the castle into a secret room only the staff know about. A room sealed by a transparent door in which to be opened you'd need a spell created by the headmaster of the school.

"Agustana Fotorum!" Professor Burton said.

The door slowly reveals itself with a small white shimmer around the creases of the door. He looks to make sure no one is around, and he goes in. He looks around and cannot find what he is looking for. His heart starts to race and then he looks to his right. On top of a very old book lies a medium sized beautiful purple stone. This stone is meant for training purposes. It will provide the user with a holographic opponent, reading their mind and using their weaknesses against them. Maybe for Aria it would be her mother. Professor

Burton was eager to see how Aria would react to this during her training. He ran to find Aria in the library reading a book about the wizards who created the school.

"Aria, can you come with me? I have something for you," he says.

She follows him to the courtyard wondering why he couldn't give her this inside.

"Here, this is a stone that will basically read your mind and find your weaknesses and you must fight your weaknesses. Keep in mind that you may have to fight more than one at a time. Any time you wish to stop, just grab the stone and shut the top of it. Give it a go," Professor Burton suggested.

Aria opens up the stone and lets it read her mind. What would happen next was confusing for Professor Burton. Aria's greatest weaknesses were nowhere near what he had assumed them to be. It wasn't her mother, it wasn't her father, and it wasn't being alone on this crazy journey. Her greatest weakness was love. All the people she loved had come out of the stone, one of them being Professor Burton. He grabs the stone and he shuts it.

"May I ask what exactly your weakness is?" he asked.

"Are you sure you really want to know?" Aria chuckled.

"Yes, I do," he replies.

"Love, professor. My father can easily distract me. He knows me like the back of his hand. Come to think of it, he was never really around much. Never really made a connection with me. I want him to be amazed if it comes down to him reading my weaknesses as I will probably be able to read his as well. All my father ever did was push people away and I learned from a really young age that I wasn't going to be the same. I will fight my father, and anything I love will be here, safe, or is already gone. I intend to win even if it means his death, I will do any and everything to bring Collin home. I wouldn't worry so much if I was you, professor," she said mysteriously.

"I'm glad to hear you're learning to control yourself. When the time comes it may not be so easy," Professor Burton informs.

"You know, I believe that our minds are very very powerful. I think everyone believes in me and believes that I can win. You're like my dad professor, your thoughts count, and your doubt could be the one thing that stops me. I've believed in you and trusted you since the first day I met you. I want you to know I don't regret it," Aria said.

Professor Burton was actually pleased to see Aria like this. He handed Aria the stone and told her to practice every second she had a chance. It had been a while since Professor Burton and Professor Steven had seen each other, so he went to the hospital wing to look for Professor Steven. He looked rather shocked to see him.

"Hello professor. Before you say anything I want you to know that with or without me, Aria would still be doing this. It's better if she has someone in her corner the whole way through rather than bashing her for making her own decisions. Miss Whitlock is a very talented witch. She could probably even kick my ass," Professor Burton pleaded.

It should be known that knowing Aria was his daughter gave him some ease. He felt less threatened by the others who were trying to take on the role of a parent figure. He was quite jealous of Professor Steven, but definitely not anymore. Aria being his daughter gave him a justification for always wanting to protect her. As if he wasn't doing it for no reason, and didn't look crazy doing it either, even though no one really knew yet.

"I understand you're trying to protect her, but do you really think you can protect her from everything?" Professor Steven asks.

"I don't need to. I will protect her from whatever I can, and what I cannot, I will teach her how to protect herself. I don't want her to rely on anyone, but I want her to know when she does need the help, it will be there," he said.

Professor Burton saying this made Professor Steven realize that maybe he would be a better father figure than him. He had never thought of things this way. After all being one of the most powerful wizards of all comes an expanded mind. A mind in which Professor Burton could bewitch.

Dinner finally arrives and Aria starts walking up to the professors table.

"Hey, Aria?" Ryan calls.

"Oh, hey how are you doing?" Aria replies.

"Oh you know, same shit different day. I was wondering if you wanted to come sit with me and my brother. We would be delighted to have you," Ryan asks.

"Of course, why not," Aria replies.

Aria starts to follow Ryan and they sit at one of the tables in front of Professor Burrton. He notices Aria finally making herself some friends and is grateful. Throughout the time of their dinner they talk about their hobbies and interests as their witch and wizard careers start to begin. They got to know each other very quickly. Making friends in the world of magic happens to be a lot easier than in the non magic world.

"So can I just ask, how did you discover this place?" Ryan asks.

"Crazy story actually. Um, my mother was murdered and I was imprisoned and when I escaped I went to a library and there was a man there who I guess knew I was a witch. He was very proper and intimidating, but he left behind a paper with the address to the school and I never saw him again," Aria spat out.

Ryan could tell it was hard for Aria to talk about this so she tried to lift the mood.

"Wow, that's some stuff straight out of a movie or book or something. Word around the school is that you're a very talented one," Ryan hints.

"Yes I am, not because I'm super smart or amazing or anything. I was just born into a powerful family. I do have some pretty cool things I can do. Please tell me that's not why I'm sitting here?" Aria asks.

"No, of course not. I just felt like you would be a nice friend to have. Like I said, me and my brother keep to ourselves pretty often. We're like the eyes of the school if you want to understand it better. My brother thinks you're stunning, but don't worry he knows you're with Collin and wouldn't try anything. I've got to warn you the last girl he had feelings for lasted for a little over a year but she moved really far away with her family. She was also a mortal which my family didn't like," Ryan said.

"So if I was a mortal they wouldn't want you around me?" Aria asked.

"Correct. They're weird about that stuff. They think there isn't anything we can learn from them and that they're scared of people like us and if we make a wrong move they could try to harm us," Ryan said.

"Would you like to see something awesome?" Aria asked.

"Sure?" Ryan replied.

"Meet me in the back courtyard in an hour and you can bring Reggie as well. It's something that I'll be using to train myself. I actually got it from one of the professors. I bet you can guess which one," Aria chuckled.

"Okay cool, we'll see you then. Also hmm let me think, Professor Burton?" Ryan guessed.

"Yes, see you later," Aria laughed.

Aria was starting to feel a little better about her entire situation. She started viewing everything around her so differently at this point, and started seeing a future in the school actually. The only thing missing now was Collin. She vowed to train every second she had, she wanted her dreadful father to be the last thing that stood in the way of her happiness and she wasn't planning to let him get away with trying. Aria went to go say goodnight to Professor Burton.

"Hey professor, I just wanted to say goodnight. I actually have a question for you if you don't mind?" she asked.

"Fire away," Professor Burton replied.

"Well, technically I'm not a student here, so I was just wondering if all the rules still applied to me?" she asked.

"Which rule would we be talking about exactly?" he asked.

"I want to leave the castle tonight. I will be back by morning. There are just some things I would like to take care of,"

"You can't take care of these things during the day?" he wondered.

"No actually, it's something that needs to be done immediately," she clarified.

"Do you need any help?" he asks.

"No, this one's for me to do alone," Aria said.

"Alright, well I will see you in the morning then. Don't forget we have training to do tomorrow after dinner," Professor Burton reminded her.

"For sure, I'll see you tomorrow," Aria finished.

Aria stops by her room and once again sees the photo that the headmaster gave her of her father. Thinking it would ruin her night it didn't affect her as much as she'd thought it would. She fixes her hair and goes to the back courtyard to meet with Ryan and Reggie.

"Hey guys! Are you ready? This is super cool," Aria said, as she pulled out the stone.

"Yes we are. We almost got caught by Professor Bliss though. Couldn't imagine what she would have done if she knew we were sneaking out," Ryan said.

"What is that?" said Reggie.

"Well I'm glad you noticed. It's why you're here tonight. Professor Burton gave this to me. It's a stone that provides a version of your most sensitive thoughts and fears for you to duel with," Aria informs.

"Why would we want something like that? Isn't it bad?" Reggie asked.

"No, you see this is perfect for when I have to fight my father. What if he brings something stupid and personal into our fight. This is perfect. I thought it was really cool and wanted to share. I hope I'm not pushing because I was going to let both of you try it," Aria said.

"Nope, I'm definitely in. This looks awesome, scary, but awesome," Ryan said.

"Okay so I'm going to put it on the floor and open it. When you want to stop, just simply walk up to the stone and close it," Aria informs.

Ryan gets in her battle position as taught in class. The stone starts to light up, and out comes a black figure. Reggie nor Aria really knew what this figure represented.

"What's your worst fear?" Aria asked.

"Believe it or not I am actually terrified of snakes. I'm not sure what this was about?" Ryan said.

"Reggie, you try next. Hopefully it works this time. I'll have to ask the professor about this," Aria said.

"Okay let's do this," Reggie said.

Reggie stood in front of the stone and once again it started to light up. Finally out comes a guard from the prison Aria was kept at. Although Reggie had no idea that that's who the man was.

"Who is that?" Aria asked intensely.

"I don't know, sometimes I have dreams about these men with weird masks and some cool looking robes. Do you know this man," Reggie says.

"I-I have to go, I'm sorry," Aria says.

Aria turns around and starts running as far as she could away from the school. Now, if the situation would have been different maybe Ryan and Reggie wouldn't have done what they did next, but it looked pretty serious and they've grown to care for Aria's well being. The two ran back into the school. Knowing Aria and Professor Burton get along so well they went to him instead of someone who could have caused Aria more issues.

"Professor Burton! Listen please," Reggie said.

"What are you doing out of bed? Go now!" Professor Burton firmly said.

"No, please just listen, It's about Aria," Ryan said with hope he'd listen.

"What is it?" he asked.

"Sir, she's gone," Reggie replied.

"What the hell do you mean she's gone?" he asked.

"She was showing us the stone you gave her. She was very excited to show us, we had snuck out of the castle to the back courtyard and when Reggie used it something happened. He gets scared of this man, well men, multiple, that he has dreams of and when Aria saw the men she ran away. I don't know where she's going but she's not on school grounds anymore which means if she needs help she can't use magic without anyone seeing. I'm really worried. Please help us find her," Ryan pleaded to Professor Burton.

"Okay, I will go out and look for her. Please go to bed where you were supposed to be in the first place," Professor Burton said.

Professor Burton went to find Professor Bliss and the headmaster. There were many other professors that could stick around and watch the school.

"Professor Bliss, I need your help, Aria ran away. I would like to search the woods for her just to make sure she didn't go in there. It's fine that she left but I need to make sure she isn't hurt. Please come with me. I plan to ask William as well," Professor Burton begged.

"Very well then, I'll come. You know at some point you're going to have to tell her that she is your daughter, yes I know. You and William speak quite loudly to each other, don't you know?" Professor Bliss commented.

"I know. I just don't want to do it at the wrong moment and lose another daughter. I think about Alexia every single day, but since I found out about Aria, she's given me hope again. Please don't say anything," he asked.

"I won't but William is now at rest, me and you will have to go on alone. If you need any protection don't be scared I'm right by your side," Professor Bliss chuckled.

"Yeah right," he replied.

"How did you find out about Aria leaving tonight exactly?" she asked.

"I told them they were safe to speak with me. Those friends that Aria made before, they just ran up to me and said she was gone. She was showing them something I gave to her. I gave her the stone. Whatever is in Reggies dreams really scares Aria. I think it was the men from the prison," Professor Burton said.

"I won't say anything but we can't let the students sneak out even on school grounds. You know this," Professor Bliss said.

"I know I am sorry about that. I honestly didn't know until they came to find me to tell me about Aria. We should head out. I have a class in the morning," he said.

Professor Bliss and Professor Burton head out towards the woods. They search for about two hours before they finally agree Aria is not there. This worried Burton to his core.

"Hey don't worry, wherever she is I'm sure she's going to come back. I doubt she would just drop everything and leave. She loves you even if she doesn't know yet," Professor Bliss said as they sat down on a massive log.

"I hope you're right about that," he said, looking down at his feet in self pity.

"She will," Professor Bliss said as she kindly put her hand under Professor Burton's chin forcing him to look up.

Both of the professors are feeling many things at the moment. Burton builds up the courage to kiss Professor Bliss. It had been one of the most romantic kisses he's had in many years. Same goes for Professor Biss.

As soon as they kissed it felt like the whole world had stopped. There are problems in the magic world that are way bigger than any human could even comprehend, and now it feels like that weight is floating just above their shoulders. Dreading to let the pain flow back down, their lips separate. Staring into each other's eyes they're both curious what they've unlocked within each other. Professor Burton had never seen this coming, but on the other hand Professor Bliss has had feelings for him for a while, she just knows how to step back and wait for the right moment. If only everyone could do that.

"You never told me you felt this way. I knew we were close but I never thought. I'm quite surprised?" Professor Burton said.

"You never asked," she replied mysteriously.

"I want to pursue this, I do Nona, but I need to spend time with my only daughter. She needs to be my priority. Can we try this again when she starts going to school here maybe?" he asks.

"Of course. I'm not going anywhere, take your time. I want you to know that this will not be a repeat of your last life. Please see the beauty and transformation before you try to put yourself in a dark place. Those times weren't only hard for you. I had lost my bestfriend and he is finally starting to come back. Don't leave again," Professor Bliss replied.

Professor Burton had nodded his head with sympathy and love.

"I forgive you. Forgive yourself," Professor Bliss said as she stood up.

The professors started to walk back to the school, no sign of Aria anywhere. Professor Burton was really hoping that she would turn up the next morning. He wondered if she was thinking about him. If he was a good enough reason to come back, even though she didn't know about him yet. So where is Aria then?

Walking down the streets of England, all Aria could do was worry about this battle. She wanted it that way. She figured she might as well get it all out now, while no one is watching. Everyone knows that Aria has been through it, she wanted to keep a tough exterior not for others but for herself. Going through so much trauma can have an effect on a person, Aria wanted to be different. She wanted everyone to see that she was okay, and to stop treating her like a feather. Aria didn't run away because she was scared, she ran away because everything started to connect. After all she is a talented witch and when things start to connect that usually means really good or really bad. She knew a lot of people at the school were probably freaking out and she wanted it that way, so when she went back they would see she was fine.

Aria went to the nearest library she could find. She picked up a beautiful quill, and started thinking of names. She wanted to create some of her own spells.

"Aegisia Auspico. That could be great for a protection spell," Aria said.

Aria left the library after not being there very long and found a good spot to practice her magic.

She found a field. It was dark so no one could see her. Aria wasn't sure of how to create a spell. She was always told magic and being a magic being, is all about wanting something so badly, and then letting yourself have it. Aria loved nature and didn't like to wear shoes when she would practice. She was also told that magic can sometimes be like water, flexible. She closed her eyes and imagined what would happen when she said the words, and she sat there and thought about it until she could feel it in her heart. She pulls out her wand and slides it from her head to her toes.

"Aegisia Auspico!" she said.

Nothing had happened.

"I don't understand what I did wrong," she said looking at her wand.

Aria decides to go for a walk down a pretty street and relax a little. Beautiful lights, It had rained a little while earlier which made the streets shiny and black. It was a little chilly given Halloween was just around the corner. Walking past a bar full of regular people made her think about how different the two worlds are. Looking down to her bare feet as she walked the sidewalk, mind racing, she wasn't paying attention to what was in front of her. Aria had stepped on a piece of glass. She found a bench and sat down. When she turned her foot around to look at it she noticed there was no cut on her foot. She was amazed and understood that it had been from her spell, but she still hadn't understood what the spell actually did to her. She tried all night but couldn't figure it out. It had still hurt, but there was no physical reaction.

As for Collin he wasn't doing so good. Aria's father would only feed him once a day as he did to Aria while she was there. It helps drain their powers, which answers why Aria had felt so off in the beginning of her journey at the school. In the same spot, and the same shackles, Collin sits and waits. He's hoping that Aria comes when she said she would be back at the school, but the more days that pass the more he is unsure of it. The biggest thing he worried about was if she had found someone else.

Aria's goal was to create at least one protection spell and one offensive spell. Aria hopes to find Professor Burton taking her more seriously when she returns with these spells. She wanted the offensive spell to be something people had never seen before. Something unique, different. Aria had so many options, but none had really stuck out to her in a way where she thought she could amaze people. Then the idea popped into her head, what if she could create an animal that is meant for just her protection, somewhat of a spirit guide, but living.

"Which animal do I relate to the most though? I'm gentle, I always want to help but unfortunately I can be naive, and I believe my heart is truly pure to those who handle it with care. Aria ran as fast as she could back to the field. It was almost morning so she could not do this just yet. Believe she studied all day about it.

Back at Watford Academy, Professor Burton was awakened before most. He couldn't scratch the idea of Aria hurt somewhere on her own without anyone to help her.

Being a man who lost a lover and a child, who is given a second chance is a once in a lifetime opportunity even in the magic world. He wasn't sure how things would go with Professor Bliss after everything that had happened the night before. He decides to go let the headmaster know that Aria had parted ways, hopefully temporarily. He lets a gentle knock on the door.

"Yes come in," William says.

Professor Burton takes a few steps forward.

"What can I do for you?" William asks.

"I-um, just wanted to make sure that you were aware of Aria's departure from us last night. I'm currently unaware of when or if she will be back, nor where she is or headed. She had left with not much of any warning to anyone," he informed.

"Yes, I happen to be aware. I am extremely dedicated to my students and their safety. She had run out of the back courtyard after using that stone of yours with a couple friends she had made. I feel she will be back in a short matter of time. Perhaps she may even come back a better witch from when she parted," William said.

Ryan and Reggie started to look for the professor that morning. They felt so passionately as to barge into the headmasters office.

"Professor Burton! Please tell us you've heard from her. We miss her dearly. She's the first person that accepted my brother and I for who we truly are. We didn't have to put on a mask for her. Please? Anything?" Ryan said.

"I'm sorry, nothing just yet. Professor Longtail thinks she will be back shortly," Professor Burton replied.

"And you? What do you think? You know her best," Reggie said.

"I trust in my authority. I believe what the headmaster said is true until I am proven wrong, get to class now please," Professor Burton said, with a cold but fearful look on his face.

The day had passed quickly for everyone. William had started to realize that Aria was starting to become the heart of this school. He thought back to everything she had done for others and hadn't even become a student yet. It was just out of the pure kindness of her heart. The headmaster had started to miss her presence as well. Dinner time had finally come around.

"Hey Reggie, how was your classes?" Ryan asked Reggie.

"Actually pretty go-"

"Anyways, I have an evil plan and I want you to join me. Please?" Ryan asked.

"What is this little evil plan of yours?" Reggie replied.

"Let's go find Aria. I feel it deep down that she is close. Please? We can go tonight," Ryan pleaded.

"To risk getting expelled from school? This school is the best thing that's ever happened to us. Why risk that?" Reggie said.

"Don't you think she would do the same for us? Look, we can just look and if we can't find her we can come back," she said.

"Was not coming back also an option? I wasn't aware," Reggie chuckled.

"Oh shut up, Please?" she continued to beg.

"What if her father is around her? I can't protect either one of us from a man like that. We're too young," Reggie debated.

"First of all, if Aria has the courage to fight her own father, we should have the courage to go look for her. Plus I heard he's in The D2, so we're safe," Ryan pleaded again.

"What's a D2? A prison?" Reggie asked.

"No dummy, It's another dimension. Do you not listen to any of the school dramas? I tend not to include myself but I definitely listen. Her father is in a dimension right above ours. Aria is a speed traveler. So any fighting will most likely be there, Please?" Ryan begged once more.

"Fine, but I want to be back by morning with no exceptions. We seriously can't get expelled or I may lose it," Reggie agreed.

"YES! Okay thank you. I love you so much," Ryan let out a laugh.

"I love you too," Reggie smiled.

A few hours later the siblings found themselves tip-toeing through the halls of the castle dodging every professor they found. Then they find themselves face to face with Professor Burton, and as much as they trust him when it comes to Aria, they know where his loyalties lie, and that would be with the headmaster.

"Professor Burton, I have one thing to say to you at this very moment," Ryan said.

"What would that be?" he sarcastically replied.

"Slumporium!" she yelled as she had pulled out her wand without Professor Burton noticing.

"What the hell? If we don't get kicked out for leaving we're definitely getting kicked out for this, are you nuts!" Reggie angered.

"Are you kidding me? Stop acting like a baby. I'll take the heat if that happens. Now shut up and let's go before I have to do that again," Ryan demanded.

The siblings did as they said they would and looked as far around England as they could. Not being able to find her they found themselves exhausted and physically drained. They decided to find some nearby land to have a sit, and then head back to Watford Academy. Excited to finally sit down and stop walking they found a field to sit at. Aria on the other hand was still walking the streets trying to decide what animal she wanted to create. Aria goes back to her original training field.

"What the hell?" Aria shockingly says.

"Oh my gosh Aria!! Where the hell have you been? We have literally been looking for you everywhere. I had to cast a sleep spell on Professor Burton for this moment!" Ryan said enthusiastically.

"I know I'm sorry. It's really hard to explain but I can't come back yet. You can't stay here with me. I miss both of you terribly. You have to go back now, I will be coming back soon but don't tell anyone that I'm coming. Please, give me your word," Aria said.

"Yes, yes of course. We would never," Reggie said.

"Good, I need you to relay a message for me. To Professor Burton. Please tell him I'm okay. He doesn't need to know how you know but please tell him. I have absolutely zero idea why, but I can feel his pain since I've left, his sadness. Please tell him to stop feeling that way," Aria asked.

"Of course. If we don't get expelled we will definitely relay the message. We miss you Aria, please come back to us soon," Ryan said.

"I could probably be back in a couple days but Professor Burton needs to relax," Aria said.

They both gave Aria a loving hug, and were satisfied knowing that Aria was somewhere dead. They managed to sneak back into the school and get back in bed the same way that they had parted. They could both use some rest after a wild night as such. The next morning finally came around and they were summoned to the headmaster's office as they assumed they'd be. They slowly made their way there, not only because they were terrified of what was about to happen, but because they felt they could barely walk. They finally get there and share a guilty but honest look.

"Would you like to explain to Professor Burton and I why he, how should I put it, dozed off, during his shift last night?" Professor Longtail asks.

"Yes um, we're terribly sorry for that, but you have to trust we had good reason. We actually relay a message. From, Aria," Ryan said.

"What are you talking about?" Professor Burton said intensely.

"She wants me to tell you, professor, that she is safe and she will be home soon. She also said to tell you to stop being so depressed because she can feel it and it's stopping her from doing what she needs to do, and the longer it takes her to do whatever it is that she's doing, the longer it'll take for her to come home," Reggie said.

Professor Burton and Professor Longtail share a concerning look.

"How do you know this?" Professor Longtail asked.

"We just know, professor. It's not our place to share how we know, but we would never lie about this, we care about Aria and Aria cares for you as if you were her father. I promise we wouldn't mislead you. Please don't expel us," Ryan begged.

"Go to class. Professor Burton and I need to talk in private," Professor Longtial said.

"What is it, William," Professor Burton said.

"I wanted to see how you were holding up. I know this being not the most craved of situations," Professor Longtail asked.

"I'm alright, I just don't want to lose her as I believe I have said again and again. I don't mean to be such a fool but I can't help it sir. She means everything to me," Professor Burton stated in a monotone attitude.

"I believe she will come. You must have patience. I ask you to continue teaching your classes. In the meantime I'm sure you will admire the company of Nona," William says as he winks at Professor Burton.

"Sir, but how do you-"

"I know everything that happens in or around my school professor. I don't believe I have told you this as much as I'd like to, but you have been a faithful professor as you have a friend. It joys me to see you happy once more. Given a second chance. My advice to you, don't take advantage of it and do not let anyone know your next moves," William speaks.

"Thank you. I shall get going, as you are aware I have a class of first years this morning," Professor Burton said.

Aria sat down in the same spot for many hours trying to figure out what she did to herself. She wondered if maybe, just maybe, if she hurt herself again she would be able to figure it out. She wandered to a nearby local shop called "Silly Goose", and had purchased a vintage pocket knife.

"Hello, I'm looking for something that only does little damage, something simple," Aria asked the man.

"I have just the thing you seek madam. Chester Wildrof at your service young lady. How do you do?" Chester asked.

"I'm good, just finding my way and getting things done as they say," Aria replied with a faint smile on her face.

"Wonderful. Is there a specific color you may seek? We have red, blue, black, green, purple, and yellow?" Chester asked.

"Black please," Aria answered.

"Very well. That would be thirty pounds please," Chester said.

"Thank you sir, have a wonderful day," Aria said.

Aria started to walk back to her everyday spot where she could continue in private. She put her little bag down and took out the knife. Aria continued to open it, and out comes a shiny blade, very bright and silver with designs such as swimming blades. Aria puts the tip of the knife to the tip of the pointer finger on her left hand and lightly drags the knife down. Just enough to do as much damage as if you were to scrape your knee. Then it hit her.

Aria Whitlock had created a protection spell in which one could cast upon oneself to endure the pain mentally but not physically. If she were to break her arm for example she would feel the pain of the break but endure no physical pain and her arm would not actually be broken.

"Oh my God," she quietly whispers to herself.

In a panic but excited and amazed manner Aria shoots up and starts laughing. Such a sweet and innocent laugh. Twirling around in circles. After Aria's fun time she came back down to reality, and had wished Professor Burton was there to see her accomplish such a task. She wanted to go back to the castle and continue her training, but she wanted to create something amazing, never seen before, before she could do so. She decided to go to the library just down a small road. Aria had the intention to research different mythological creatures and create one herself but with a little twist.

The first creature she had researched was a phoenix. Some of these birds are very rare to find, although that intrigued Aria, she did not believe a bird would suit her. It needs to be an animal that represents who she is. The next animal she researched was a Dragon. Any kind, any sort. This is a creature of bravery, honesty, and dedication. These may have also described Aria, but a dragon can be known for its anger and/or aggression as well. Anger and aggression is something that has never really possessed Aria. Not yet. The final animal researched happened to be a pegasus. A pegasus can represent loyalty, honor, immortality, and are usually always eager to help. A very gentle creature indeed.

Aria waited long before the night had arrived, but by the time it had come Aria had fallen asleep. At the brisk of dawn she had awoken and it was her last chance before daylight that she could do what she had so craved to do. This is a moment she has been waiting for a very long time. She pulls out her wand.

"Although I may not be worthy of your services, I create you to serve and to protect me. Only me. I will honor you and be loyal to you and care for you to the best of my ability. You are kind, you are gentle, but show no mercy to those who hurt me or my loved ones unless I give the order. When I snap my fingers you will appear, you will know when to disappear. I will call upon you for services not only to protect me, but because as of tonight you are my family and we will spend time together and build love. You are one of the most intelligent creatures on the planet. You are made of fire and love. Your name is Nuri. You are a king, but a gentleman," Aria casted her wand, as she traced a life size pegasus before her.

Aria had hoped to get what she asked for and she did. A pegasus, on fire, standing before her eyes.

"Hello? Can we communicate," Aria said.

"Yes we can, but only telepathically, and not often but I will always be able to understand you," Aria hears a deep but godly voice in her head.

"Well I'll probably eventually be able to change that. Do you understand why I created you?" Aria asks.

"Protection, loyalty, love, master," Nuri says.

"There will come a time when I need to battle someone close to me. When this time may come I need you to stay safe okay?" Aria asks.

"Understood. May I ask a question, master?" Nuri asks.

"Of course, anything," Aria replies.

"Why Nuri? Are you aware that someone in your life may have this name as well? You created me to be one of the smartest animals on the planet and created me with intellect, so I may be able to see the future in certain situations. I hope that may be of service to you," Nuri says.

"It surely will when I ask for it. I am trying to do everything on my own and I believe it will make me stronger. Please don't help me unless I ask for it. Never forget you are not only a servant and not only a friend, but my family. Nuri happens to be a name describing what you are. You are light, and fire my friend. I believe it is perfect. Now tell me, is it safe for me to ride you?" Aria asked.

"Of course it is. Just tell me where you want to go and we'll be there in a flash," Nuri said.

"Alright, are you aware of the Watford Witchcraft and Wizardry School?" she asks.

Nuri nods his head.

"I need to go there in the morning, but first we need to find a cool outfit, and I could braid your hair if you like. Along the way we can talk about how we are going to enter the school, it will be so awesome Nuri. I fancy seeing Professor Burton again. I miss him," Aria said.

Nuri nods his head again. Aria hops on him and they begin the journey to find Aria a cool outfit for when she arrives back at school. They talk about how they are going to enter the grounds of the castle as she braids Nuri's hair. Aria hadn't mentioned this to Nuri, but he already knew that she does not want to do this to look cool, she fancies to prove herself to those around and to herself that she can make it on her own with a little courage and dedication.

Back at the school Professor Burton wakes up for his final shift to monitor the hallways before sunrise. He wanders the halls hoping Aria would come back during the first half of the day as he has dismissed two of his classes. Just by a glance you could tell he wasn't getting any good sleep since she left, but he had to take the advice of Ryan and Reggie and not stand in Aria's way with his emotions. Was Aria fighting someone? Was she safe? Is she eating? Those are some of the questions he fancied answers to.

Ryan and Reggie happened to already be awake. They had suspected today would be the day Aria had returned but they were not completely sure of it, though they would be ready. They also happened to be excited because it was the one day in the week they do not get homework, which is on Fridays. Eventually it becomes time for breakfast. All the students had come and sat down ready for their day to start. It's been oddly quiet around the school since Aria left, everyone is starting to believe she may be the heart of the school. The headmaster had been aware of this as well and had an amazing opportunity for Aria.

Aria and Nuri found some clothes that make both of them look amazing. Like they've known each other a lifetime which is how it felt between the two. Aria had put on a beautiful black two piece. A laced black top, which was see through everywhere but her breasts, it was tight to her skin and long sleeved with black lace. The bottom half was like a long skirt torn down the side starting from her hip. Aria had braided her and Nuri's hair. Nuri got a magic black saddle which would never fall off unless Aria herself took it off. Aria had also done her makeup. She loved this new identity of herself. It made her feel confident and strong and beautiful, not to mention.

The time had finally arrived. Aria and Nuri started to head for the front of the school. The fields around the school were so big. Aria got off of Nuri and told him to go. He knew exactly what to do. Aria had slowly walked a little closer to the school and people sitting by some windows had noticed and ran into the dining hall to let everyone know she had returned. This made Professor Burton's heart drop. He shared a look with William and stood up. Everyone started running as fast as they could to get outside and see what had happened to her, but she stayed at a distance. Aria then finally meets her eye with the only person she wanted to see. Ryan and Reggie were so excited they tried to run up to Aria, but Aria held up her hand and pushed them back safely.

Awaiting everyone to come outside it had finally happened. Holding her hands behind her back so no one could see or hear she snaps her fingers and Nuri on fire, in which he can control, appears right by her side. She puts her hand on his snout and hugs his head from the side. Pegasus are not very common in their specific world of magic, so everyone stood still, shocked and amazed that she could tame an animal as such. Aria gets on Nuri.

"Take me over there please, make it look good," Aria whispers.

Nuri brings Aria right in front of Professor Burton. She gets off of Nuri.

"Hi, I'm here to say that I need you to trust me, we need to have a better understanding that I can take care of myself more than you think I can," Aria said in front of everyone.

"Is that why you left? Because of me?" Professor Burton asked.

"No, but I need you to say you will start having a lot more faith in me than you have before I left," Aria said.

"I promise. I don't want to lose you again," Professor Burton whispers in her ear.

"Thank you! I um- I love you," Aria anxiously says.

Professor Burton's life flashes before his eyes, but he did not fancy making a fool out of himself or Aria. So in front of the whole school and staff standing outside.

"I love you too," he says.

Everyone outside starts cheering for Aria.

"Where did you get the pegasus?" The headmaster asks.

"That is a great question. I was waiting on it actually. I created it with magic. It is a part of me. He is the most loyal companion I've had in a long time. I love him dearly," Aria states.

"Does it have a name?" the headmaster asks, standing in the middle of a line of the staff.

"Yes, his name is Nuri, he represents fire and light. I believe he deserves the name because in my time of darkness he was my light. I talk to him so much and he keeps all my secrets. We're a really good team together," Aria stated.

The headmaster and Professor Burton share a look. William nods his head in hopes Professor Burton will share his name finally with not only Aria but everyone standing there.

"Where did you come up with the name?" Professor Burton asks.

"I came across the definition of the word while I was in the library, researching which animal I wished to create. Is something wrong?" Aria asks.

Before the professor could say anything Nuri bumps into Aria.

"Remember what I told you? About someone in your life already having this name? I am honored to share it with someone who will be in your life a long time," Nuri telepathically communicates.

"Wait a second, that's your name isn't it? Nuri? I had no idea. That's quite amazing," Aria states.

Aria gives Professor Burton a hug, he has no words left to speak. He stands quietly as a proud and accomplished father. Aria hops on Nuri and walks up to Ryan and Reggie.

"Who's first?" Aria asks.

The two start pushing each other like any normal brother and sister would. Of course being the woman, Ryan got on Nuri first, and they went on such an amazing ride.

"This is so much better than a broom!" Ryan shouts.

"I know right! This is bloody amazing!" Aria shouts back.

"Can I ask if you're alright," Ryan asks.

"Never better!" Aria shouts back.

Aria and Ryan's ride had finally come to an end.

"Reggie, it's so amazing you're going to love it. You can feel the wind in your hair and you don't have to worry constantly about falling off as you would a broom!" Ryan said.

"Hey, Aria, I actually have a class to get to about now. Rain check?" Reggie flirtatiously asked.

"Definitely," Aria replied.

It still feels very weird for Aria to be at the castle without Collin. He wonders if he is still even alive. Aria had a feeling he was, but what would her father need with Collin? It was a nice and shiny day for Aria to practice, but it seems Professor Burton had something else in mind considering he canceled two of his morning classes.

"Aria, I know you have a lot to do but I was wondering if you'd follow me?" he asks.

"Yes of course, you're not going to kill me or anything right?" Aria chuckled.

"No, I just wasn't sure if you were really eating whilst you were away. I figured you'd fancy something other than what they normally serve at school. After all, we can create anything. I arranged a picnic for myself and you and your two friends Ryan and Reggie," Professor Burton stated while walking.

"I thought Reggie had a class just now?" Aria asked.

"Indeed he did, but I also arranged for him to be excused. He was told where to go, I assume he should be there by now," he replies.

Aria and Professor Burton continue to walk to one of the smaller outside areas of the school and just as he said a beautiful picnic had been arranged and better yet, they actually waited for Aria to start eating. Aria appreciated it so much, she gave Professor Burton a big hug, it lasted so long she started to not want to let go.

"Why?" Aria broke down into tears.

"What are you speaking of?" he asked, confused.

"Why do you keep doing these nice things for me? Do you pity me? Or my life perhaps?" she asked.

"No, no, please don't be misled by the ideas whirling around in that amazing brain of yours. I'm just a nice guy, and you have been very nice to me and I bet the entire school can agree, so what's wrong with me being nice to you? Ever since we met you have changed me for the better," he said.

"Thank you, professor," Aria replied.

All four of them sit down at the table and begin to have some of the delicious food that Professor Burton has provided for them. He was right when he said Aria hadn't eaten a whole lot. He had never seen her eat so happily and so quickly. Although she may not know that he is her real father, he definitely feels the time to tell her is on the horizon.

"Can you believe she did that?" Professor Longtail asks.

"Yeah, no, that was quite something," Professor Bliss replies.

"You seem a bit off, could it be about what happened between you and Nuri in the forest the night Aria left?" Professor Longtail questioned.

"I knew you saw that. I still don't understand how you see everything that goes on around here. Yes, it is about that. I have been waiting for him to come around for such a long time, and then Aria just comes around like she owns the place and takes the spotlight off of me. You know, I used to be the most beautiful person in this school until she came," Professor Bliss replies.

"Perhaps that may be your ego talking. You do know he is her father correct?" he replies.

"I don't care. When I want someone's attention I get it, and I get it the way I want. If it wasn't for me she'd probably be dead by now," she said.

"Why do you say such a thing," he asked.

"Oh bugger off, you don't actually care. I must go now because I have class that I don't really want to teach," she pleads.

The headmaster notices the behavior of Professor Bliss immediately, and calls all the other professors in without letting her know.

"I'm going to need all of you to keep an eye on Nona. She has been acting quite strange," he warns.

"However so?" Professor Steven asks.

"She lets off being jealous of Aria. She just left the office and she seemed upset so I asked her why and she said that ever since Aria came into the picture she has stolen her so-called spotlight. Honestly I always thought the so-called spotlight was on you Nuri. You have been one of the toughest wizards to figure out, before Aria came. I just need you guys to make sure Nona doesn't give Aria any advice that could hurt her or put her in danger. If so should happen, because Aria is yet a child we would need to get the Ghostly Provence involved. I'm not sure how long endangering a young witch would be at the Gonstroon Prison," The headmaster states.

"I remember when I was young and I first heard of the Gonstroon Prison. I didn't take it seriously actually, thought it was quite a funny name, but then I saw one of the guards. They were looking for someone and I vowed never to let myself see one again. I heard you can't even hurt the guards there because they're ghosts, and they can make you walk right into the prison yourself," Professor Steven says.

"I'm not so sure if that's how it works but they definitely are not something to mess with. They love to give out the death penalty, or life for that matter. We just have to keep a close eye," Professor Longtail said.

Aria had really missed school while she was gone. Although she wasn't a student yet, that didn't really stop her.

"Professor Burton?" Aria speaks.

"Pleasure, what can I do for you?" he replies.

"Well I just wanted to say I know you have been teaching two classes lately, your class, and then potions for Professor Bliss. I wanted to show you and the headmaster something I created that I think you both might find very useful in and out of school. Is there a time the three of us could get together?" Aria asked.

"I will have you summoned to his office after this class if that's alright," Professor Burton informs.

"Yes, that would be fine. I look forward to seeing you again," Aria concludes.

Professor Burton had just been missing out on one thing, Aria was planning to see the headmaster immediately. She would be there long before him actually. Aria makes her way to his office and gets ready to knock on the door, but it appears there is someone in there already.

"But sir, I really need you to be aware! Someone in the school is working for him, please! I never talk to anyone, I'm all eyes and ears. I would know this better than anyone! Someone is after that girl and they're here!" a mysterious voice said.

"I will consider it. I won't falsely accuse my staff of such things. We have all grown to care for the girl and it is hard to fake that," Professor Longtail replied.

Aria had felt a little guilty for eavesdropping so she had finally knocked on the door before she was to hear something she would regret.

"May I come in. It's important," Aria said.

"Of course, this is Theodore Villa. He is the groundskeeper at our school, but everyone calls Theo,"

"Nice to meet you sir, it's always a pleasure to meet a friend of a friend, no matter the age," Aria said.

"I will leave you two alone, we will have to talk again at some point. Professor," he nods his head.

Aria was quite nervous to do what she was about to do. She wasn't sure if she would be getting Professor Burton in trouble so she just wanted to be honest and hope for the best.

"Professor, I would like to jump to the point. I heard what he just said, and I believe he is right. Look, you can't say where you've heard this from, but Professor Burton has been covering Professor Bliss's classes for a while now. I'm not sure what that is all about. I was aware he told you, but I wasn't sure if you knew it was still going on," Aria said.

"I'll have to take that up with him, but I appreciate your concern," he replied.

"Yes but you see, professor, something has just seemed off with her lately. She used to be really supportive of me and one day she just started ignoring me, and this even before I ran away. I regret to inform you I have kinda lost my comfort around her. I do not intend to act like a child but please tell her to keep her distance from me," she said.

The two talked and talked for a long while. Catching up on lots of missed things, and lots of personal things. Before they even know it Professor Burton knocks on the door. He is the only one that knocks on the headmaster's door only two times.

"May I," he asks.

"Yes, yes, come in come in," Professor Longtail replies.

"So, Aria, what brings us to you on this lovely day?" Professor Burton asks.

"Okay, this might sound crazy, but I have created a spell in which you do not see it, but it's like there is an invisible border between your skin and the world. It's called 'Aegisia Auspico'. I casted this upon myself and let's say I were to trip and skin my knee. With this spell I will feel the pain I would feel, but physically there is no harm. It wears off over time but I'm not sure if it's because of time, or because it's gotten too much damage and it wore out," Aria informed.

Aria picked up her wand and casted the spell upon herself once more to make sure it was still effective. She then walked up to the headmaster's desk and picked up the sharpest thing she could find, a half sword actually. She sat down and pulled up the bottom half of her beautiful skirt. She takes the sword and cuts her knee deep enough to need stitches, but when the two finally look back at her knee there is nothing there. They both look at her like she is insane, but in a good way. Professor Burton knew she was gonna do amazing things in the school, but he never assumed it would be this early, or this proficient.

"Aria, wow, I had no idea. Is this, and Nuri what you were working on while you were away?" Professor Longtail asks.

"Yes sir. I actually wanted to ask you something," she replies.

"Go for it," he chuckles back.

"I'm not sure how likely this will be, but I wanted to ask. My parents were stuck working and going to school the mortal way, but I want to grow up in the world of magic. This life has many dangers, yes, but I also believe it has many blessings. It could be people or places or things. I guess I just wondered, if I was a good enough witch do you think perhaps I could seek employment here when I am older? Even just cleaning or something to be able to take care of myself now that I'm alone?" Aria asked.

"What do you think, Professor?" Professor Longtail says.

"I think that should be fine. If anything I'm sure there are many people around the school who would help her. I think it's a good opportunity for a growing witch," he replies.

They all come to an agreeable conclusion on that matter. Aria takes a little stroll out to one of the school's gardens. It makes her think of Collin. Although it wasn't his choice it honestly feels like he's a stranger once more.

Aria wondered if he'd be the same when he got back to the school. That was if he actually came back. The headmaster had notified the parents right away but they didn't seem to care seeing they haven't bothered to come here at all.

"I know that if I was in charge of things everyone would be safe and not only that, everyone would learn how to defend themselves," Aria muttered.

"Hey, not sure who you're talking to but you looked like you needed a friend," Reggie appeared.

"Oh, hi, how are you? How is Ryan?" Aria asked.

"She's good. How are you?" Reggie replied.

"I'm doing alright. I just feel like I have more purpose and more of a reason for being in this school at this time but I don't understand what it is. Ever since I got here I felt like I was supposed to be amazing. As if it was what people expected of me, it's just been a little overwhelming but don't worry I'm not going to run off again," Aria stated.

"Do you mind if I take you up on that raincheck? I've gotten all my work done and I happen to be done with classes early today?" Reggie asks,

"Sure, let's go to the front of the school, I'll get Nuri to meet us there," she replied.

The two strolled and talked about their worries all the way until they got to the front of the school.

"Thanks for doing this with me," Aria said.

"Oh it's alright, I know a great spot where we can go," Reggie replied,

Reggie had taken Aria to an amazing spot. It was an open forest with big beautiful trees, and cute little animals. Aria had never been more flabbergasted by nature than this. There were pink and blue tiny flowers on ropes of vine everywhere. Reggie had already been there and set up a platonic date for the two of them. Aria had never noticed but Reggie was always around her, lurking in the background; not in a creepy way, but more of a protective way. Reggie did not want to disrespect her relationship with Collin, but that never meant he couldn't take care of her.

"This is so beautiful. How did you even manage to do all this? How did you get over here before?" Aria asked.

"Well I have a broom and I'm a wizard, but it's definitely not as good as Nuri," Reggie chuckled.

Reggie and Aria started to eat the food on the picnic blanket. Aria would give Nuri some every few bites. Aria was so happy at this moment it felt like all her problems were on a pause. She felt all the weight just lift off her shoulders.

"Can I tell you something?" Reggie says.

"Well of course, did you expect me to say no after all this?" Aria laughs.

"Well I just wanted to say that I know you're with Collin, and I would never want to disrespect that, ever. I just want you to know I fancy you. A lifetime. Sometimes even in the mortal world, when you meet that one specific person you just know. I'm not sure what's going on with Collin, but I want you to know I will always be there for you," Collin said with full on eye contact.

"Thank you, Reggie. I understand completely. I felt me and Collin were moving too fast, but before I could mention anything he was kidnapped by my father. Part of me thinks I owe him my life, but another part of me desires more. I'm kind of stuck at the moment but I'm sure everything will unfold itself. I appreciate everything you're doing for me, seriously," Aria replied.

They sat and talked for hours and completely lost track of time. Before they even knew it, it was already night. It was after hours at the school and they knew they were in trouble. They hop on Nuri and they get back to the school as fast as they can. They were finally back in the school, and almost near the dining room which is close to Aria's room, a wand with light at the tip of it appeared and was not a good sign.

"What the bloody hell are you two doing out this late? It is 10pm, where were you two?" Professor Burton said aggressively.

"Look, we're sorry. We were out and we lost track of time, it's my fault. Nuri was with us, we were safe. Please don't worry," Aria said.

"Aria, you are never safe, Reggie, go to bed. Aria come with me,"

Reggie gave Aria a hug and went straight to bed. Professor Burton decided to have a talk with Aria while walking her to her room.

"What were you thinking? Aria if your fathers men can catch Collin off guard they can do it to you too. All you have to do is be in the wrong place at the wrong time. Also, might I remind you although he's not here you are committed to Collin," Professor Burton said.

"I know, but Collin is starting to feel like a stranger and things between him and I started moving really fast. I just feel like so much is happening that I'm not getting the chance to be a child anymore. Reggie took me on a platonic date. Just friends. He really likes me and I like him too, but I would never do that to Collin. It kind of hurts that you think so low of me," Aria emotionally said.

At that very moment Aria had said the one thing Professor Burton never wanted to hear her say. He felt awful that Aria had begun to feel stripped of a childhood.

"Why don't you go to bed and come to my classroom in the morning. We can talk about this then. Aria, goodnight. One day you'll know why I'm so strict and protective with you,"

"Thanks goodnight," she replied.

"Until tomorrow," he winked and walked away.

The next day felt quick to come to Aria. She was nervous about what Professor Burton might say to her.

He was really mad the night before, but it was unlike him to just let her go. Aria got out of bed and did her hair beautifully, maybe this would distract Professor Burton seeing Aria has always had the most beautiful hair in their community. She sat down on her bed for a moment and thought about her entire journey so far. She wasn't sure whether the journey was coming to an end or just beginning, but either way, she was starting to feel happy and powerful. Aria made her way down to Professor Burton's classroom.

"Hi professor," Aria said.

"Morning, you look beautiful. I just wanted to talk to you about when you were away shall I call it that. You've been very different since you've come home and I just wanted to make sure that nothing bad happened to you?" he asked.

"Home?" she innocently replied.

"Yes Miss Whitlock, home," he said.

"Well nothing bad happened, something good actually. I grew up a little, and I realized that part of me growing up is needing to be more of an observer. More than anything else. When we shut our mouths and open our eyes and ears, it seems we tend to learn even more. I'm glad I realized this at a young age," Aria replied.

"Well I'm glad to hear it. Would you be alright to do some more training later after dinner?" Professor Burton asked.

"Of course, I will meet you in the courtyard tonight. I must go, unfortunately. I have some things I'd like to do," Aria said.

"See you later," he replied.

Aria nodded her head and continued herself out of the room. She wished to find Reggie. She looked for him for about thirty minutes before she finally saw him outside with Ryan.

"Hey guys, how are you Ryan, I feel like it's been forever," Aria giggled.

"I'm good, just with this one until my next class," Ryan pointed at Reggie.

"Do you have any classes soon?" Aria asked Reggie.

"Not until this afternoon. Fancy some breakfast?"

"Sure, let's go. Are you coming Ryan?"

"Duh," she replied.

The three walked to the dining area, and sat down to eat. They had a fun time just sitting and talking, catching up. Aria told them about her entire journey while she was away from the school. They were quite amazed as well. Time had passed and Aria was feeling a bit thirsty from all the breakfast food. She took a sip of her drink. A few moments later she started to feel tingling in her hands. She wasn't sure if it was her speed traveling power or if it was something she had eaten or drank.

Aria then collapsed to the floor with no warning, in front of everyone at breakfast including the staff.

"Oh my God, PROFESSOR STEVEN!!!!!!!!," Reggie screamed.

The professor had not been in the dining hall yet that day. All of the other professors had rushed over and Professor Burton had sat down and put her head on his lap. Professor Longtail went to fetch Professor Steven, and Professor Bliss was nowhere to be found. The headmaster and Professor Steven had finally arrived.

"I'm here, I'm here. You're going to need to open her mouth so I can pour this in," Professor Steven informed Professor Burton.

"What is that?" he replied.

"It's a potion that will eliminate any poisons, and temporarily put her powers on pause until she gets it out of her system by using the restroom. This is the only I can use because I'm not sure yet if she was poisoned or if this being caused by her powers. I mean, we all know she can do amazing things so it could be her powers getting to be too much for her body to keep up with. She will feel the need to use the restroom the second she wakes up, but she may not wake up right away. We need to get her to my wing immediately," he replied.

Professor Burton was very scared but he picked Aria up and ran her all the way to the hospital wing on his own. He needed to get her there fast. He does not plan to lose another child. He places Aria on one of the beds, and places her head on a pillow.

"Linol, you have to do something I can't lose another-" he then stops and catches himself about to say something he didn't want to.

Professor Steven is already aware that Aria is his daughter, how could he not after Professor Burton just said what he said.

"You just have to do something," Professor Burton said.

"Look, I'm sorry, but I have done what I can and now it's up to her to fight from the inside. She is a strong girl I'm sure she'll pull through, just like her father," he winks at the professor.

"How did you know?" Professor Burton asks.

"How could I not?" Professor Steven replies.

"How long do you think it will take for her to wake up? I mean it should be today right? She's not in a coma or anything right?" he asks.

"It's not easy for me to say until she wakes up, I truly apologize for this. Are you aware of Professor Bliss's whereabouts?" Professor Steven asks.

"I'm not sure, I haven't seen her all morning. I don't think she is even at the school. Why?" he replies.

"Curious. I'm sure you have some things to attend to, I assure you Aria will be safe with me. I won't leave her side," he replies.

"Thank you. Please don't let anyone near her other than Ryan and Reggie until I get back," Professor Burton says.

“Of course,” Professor Steven replies.

Professor Burton immediately stormed himself to the headmaster’s office. He was as furious as he was worried. He bursts through the door, without a single care given.

“I know it was her. She did this to my daughter. I want her in the Gonstroon Prison immediately. I will not allow her to be in the same building as my daughter,” he furiously, aggressively yells.

“I understand your frustrations, but it has come to me that we have no proof. I’m so sorry Nuri,” the headmaster says.

“No, I will not stand for it. One of these two are leaving the school and if it’s not her it will be Aria as well as me and I will not come back until she is gone, so I suggest the school does their best to figure this out,” Professor Burton says.

All of a sudden a small knock is frictioned with the headmaster’s door.

“Come in,” the headmaster said.

“Ah hello, what is it that I can do for you Rosalie?” he asks.

“I just wanted to come here and say I’m sorry for what happened to Aria, it was my fault,” Rosalie sadly said.

“What are you talking about,” Professor Burton questions,

“Well I saw someone putting something in her drink before she went there. I was scared to say anything, but

Aria fixed my broken hand like it was nothing and I figured I'd come here and make it up to her," she said.

"Who was it?" the headmaster asks.

"Will I get in trouble?" Rosalie questions.

"Not if you're being truthful.

"It was Professor Bliss, I'm sorry I don't want her to hate me but if I would have done something before Aria even got there she wouldn't be in this mess. My humblest apologies sir," Rosalie concluded, and left the room.

"A witness. Isn't that good enough to get her out of the school. I don't even care much at this point as long as she is nowhere near Aria ever again," Professor Burton said.

"It should be enough if Rosalie is willing to testify in front of the governed magic committee. I will speak to her as soon as I talk to Professor Bliss and the committee," William said.

"Thank you sir, I will be with Aria so I will be canceling my classes until she wakes up. It's not an option so I hope you approve or you'll have to teach my classes," Professor Burton said.

The headmaster takes some time to get a hold of the committee. For a situation as serious as this had been, they had preferred themselves to come to the school and hear the testimony with Professor Bliss in the room. The only thing left is convincing Rosalie to do it in front of the professor. William ordered her back to his office at once to speak with Rosalie about the matter.

"I wish to know if you'd be willing to tell the committee this, but the only downside is you'd have to do it in front of Professor Bliss as well? If you do this she could be taken to prison and she would not be able to bother you any longer. I need to know immediately," he said.

"I mean of course. I truly care for Aria after what she did for me. Professor Bliss doesn't scare me but being kicked out of school does," Rosalie replied.

"I can assure you as your headmaster that would not happen. I would actually bring praise upon you for doing such things. So can I bring them here before lunch?" he asks.

"Yes, sir. Just let me know when you need me," Rosalie says.

The headmaster gets the committee to the school as fast as he can. Hoping to find Nona, he is left defeated, and she's nowhere to be found. William assumes it's because she knew she was about to go to prison and left, but he hoped she'd be back and he could secretly notify the authorities from Gontroon Prison. Rosalie and Professor Burton are immediately notified to make their way back down to the headmasters office.

"Welcome, these are some of the main people from the committee. They're here to hear your testimony against Professor Bliss. Are you alright with this?" William asks.

"Yes, all I saw was she put something in Aria's drink but I was too scared to say anything because I didn't want to get in trouble. Aria fixed my broken hand for me a while back so I will do what I can to help her. I think Professor Bliss could potentially be dangerous," Rosalie testified.

"What's your role in all of this professor?" Larkin Atarof said.

"She's my daughter. It's a very complicated situation that has nothing to do with this," Professor Burton says.

"I too believe Nona has been acting strange lately. As soon as I am able to find her can I say I'll be able to call you gentlemen?" William asks.

"We would like to meet with Aria, and then we will make our decision," Larkin said.

"Well then, follow me," William said.

The gentlemen followed the headmaster all the way to the hospital wing where Aria had been resting. She had not woken up yet, but the headmaster wanted the committee to see it for themselves.

"Is she sleeping?" Larkin asked.

"No, we're not so sure when she'll wake up. It's all up to her. She has to fight from the inside now. I wanted you to see for yourselves, the damage Nona has caused to a young girl," William said.

"Alright, if you happen to see Nona Bliss, do what you can to prevent her from leaving again and we will be here as quickly as we can," Larkin said.

Sadly everyone had gone about their days hoping for Aria to wake up except one person. Professor Burton had not left her side since she had touched the bed. He couldn't bear the thought of losing her before he could tell her that he was her real father. That night the headmaster had finally decided to tell the professor to get some rest and that he would wait by Aria until the morning. As much as the headmaster had wished that to be true, he was also very tired himself.

"Are you sure that you'll be able to stay awake William?" Professor Burton asked.

"Of course, you need to go get some sleep, and I'm sorry to say that I'm not asking. Goodnight, professor," William said.

Though the headmaster was able to stay up until about two am, he had fallen asleep. Never expecting Aria to wake up so soon he drifted off peacefully. An hour had passed and suddenly Aria slowly began to wake up.

"Wha-What's going on? Oh shoot-" Aria said.

She had left the room and darted to the bathroom as fast as she could. She had taken the longest pee she had ever experienced in her life. The headmaster had woken up to Aria being gone from the bed, thankfully she had turned the light on in the bathroom so he knew she didn't run away again. She had finally returned to the hospital room and witnessed the headmaster finally awake.

"How long have you been up?" he asked.

"Not long, I had such an urge to use the restroom it was quite weird. Have you been here, by my side, all night?" Aria asked.

"Yes. Professor Burton would not leave your side so I told him I would stay here while he got some rest," William replied.

"Why is he always so kind to me? He treats me so differently than the other students. I don't disapprove of course but there has to be some sort of reason?" she asked.

"I think that may be a question for him, but while we are throwing around questions do you remember anything from the night this all happened to you?" the headmaster asked.

"No, should I? All I remember is that I was in the dining hall with Ryan and Reggie and I was thirsty so I had taken a drink of my juice and after that I was just blacked out until now. Should I be concerned?" she asked.

"Fortunately no, but we do have to keep you at an arm's length until we can get a hold of Professor Bliss. There was a witness who claimed to see what happened and at the same time Professor Bliss had become m.i.a," William responded.

Aria had given a look of defeat. If she can let her guard down so easily in a place where she feels safe, how is she going to be able to overcome her father? She got back into bed and intended to stay there until she felt like training again.

"Goodnight, professor," she said.

"Goodnight," he replied.

"Until tomorrow," she replied.

The headmaster was confused at this point because he recognized this statement before, he just wasn't sure where he had heard it from. They both eventually fell back asleep until the morning. Aria had woken up to Professor Steven with his back turned and a clipboard in his hand.

"Ah you're finally awake after your long slumber," Professor Steven said.

"Long slumber? I've only been asleep for five hours?" she wondered out loud.

"Did you wake up during the night?" he asked.

"Yes, I went to the bathroom and chatted with the headmaster. I would like to rest now," she said.

"I would love for that to happen but first I need to see that your powers are working," he informed.

Professor Burton had just begun to show up into the room. Standing in the doorway he was relieved to see Aria awake. Aria wished to be alone at the time so using her powers she pushed him out of the room and slammed and locked the door. The professor wasn't sure why this happened, but he continued to knock on the door. She had used her powers once more to silence the knocking.

"Is that enough proof? May I rest now?" she asked.

"Go ahead. I will be back soon to check on you, and I suggest you don't pull that on me. I won't go so easy on you darling. Rest up," he said.

Professor Steven stepped out of the room to talk to Professor Burton.

"She wishes to be alone right now. She had woken up in the middle of the night and conversed with the headmaster but her powers are clearly working so I told her I would be back later to check up. No father should have to go through this, I apologize," Professor Steven said.

"No worries, as long as she's alright," Professor Burton replied.

Little did the two know that Aria just wanted to take her power nap. The girl was completely drained, what else did they expect? A few hours later Aria had finally gotten up. She had woken up to the sound of Nuri telepathically yelling at her for not letting him know what was going on. He had no idea she'd been poisoned. She had opened her eyes and he was standing right in front of her. He is a part of her so of course he felt that something had happened to her.

"Nuri, what are you doing here? I'm not sure you're safe here and if anyone tries to come for me again I don't want them to know you exist," Aria said.

"I had to come see for myself how you were doing, I can't rely on these teachers filled with emotions.

Professor Burton it was? He's just been a complete mess. I really do suggest talking to him as he remains a mess," Nuri said.

"I really missed you. What about later this evening we go out and have a picnic just me and you, like the old days right?" Aria laughed.

"I will be waiting for you in the back of the school. I'm sure no one will see," Nuri replied.

"Okay but just remember to wait until I call for you. Please," she said.

"As you wish, now go talk to him. He's talking a bunch of rubbish," Nuri replied.

Aria did as she was told and continued down to Professor Burton's classroom. Unfortunately he had a class, but that wouldn't stop him from getting in a conversation with his number one girl. He let the class continue on their own for a moment while he stepped in the hall to speak with Aria.

"How are you feeling?" he asked.

"I feel like I should be asking you this instead," Aria giggled.

"I really care about you," he said, as they shared an unknowingly silence.

"It was her, wasn't it. Professor Bliss. I wanted to let you know that I was okay and I want you to know I'm always thinking of you, but I must go at once. Something important I have to take care of," Aria stated as she stormed off.

Aria decided it was a good idea to go speak with the headmaster about this while he wasn't half asleep. She knocked on his door and was welcomed with open arms.

"What can I do for you, how are you feeling?" William asked.

"I know it was her, but what if she's not doing it for the reasons we may think?" she asked.

"What reasons are you thinking of?" he replied.

"I need a little time, but I think she's working for my father. She knew exactly what spell was put on the photo of my mother, so how could she have had nothing to do with this. I would understand if she just knew it was dark magic, but sir, she knew exactly what spell, and for a witch of her knowledge, or should I say power, she shouldn't have known sir. If you don't believe me, I won't be the one looking silly in the end," she said strongly.

"I admire your courage, and I do believe you. You have my full support but I suggest you go in stealth with this matter as it may take a couple days for you to fully heal from your little incident," he replied.

"Of course I'll try not to push myself to the edge," Aria said.

"Are you planning to continue your training before you go see your father Miss Whitlock?" he asked.

"Duh, of course. How could I not?" she replied.

The headmaster nodded at Aria and she started to leave the room. Her next stop happened to be Professor

Steven. She had marched her way down to the hospital wing and not for the last time.

"Professor?" she called.

"Yes I am in here, come in!" He shouted from the far part of the room.

"Hey professor, I was just wondering if that drink you gave me will weaken or affect my powers at all?" she asked.

"Not if you have already gone to the bathroom which I heard you had. I'm sure you'll be alright. What's going on?" he replied.

"I just wanted to make sure in case I needed to use them. I'm quite glad I made a full recovery, I'm really going to need it. Thank you for helping me. I really appreciated it," she said.

"Of course, you're part of our family now and we will do what it takes to protect each other. I have some work to do so I'll need you to excuse me, but if you have any other questions, hesitate to ask," he replied.

Aria had slept through breakfast so it had become time for lunch. She took a deep breath before walking into the dining hall as she had known she was the number one conversation starter. She was expecting everyone to just stare at her, but little did she know Professor Burton wasn't going to let that happen. She walked into the room to find everyone going about their business, except two people. Ryan and Reggie. They had run up to her as fast as they could and shared a group hug.

"We missed you so much, we thought something had happened to you. We are so happy to see you standing here right now," Ryan said.

"Yeah!" Reggie said.

"Don't worry I missed you guys too, but I have something to tell you guys something super messed up," Aria replied.

"What, what is it," Reggie said.

"Professor Bliss did that to me. She poisoned my drink. I'm okay now, but I think she's working for my father. The headmaster agrees but he wants me to continue my training before I try to find her. She's probably with my father as we speak," Aria said.

"That's insane, we're so sorry," Ryan said.

"Any word from Collin lately?" Reggie asked.

"No, I really don't understand what's happened to him," she answered.

"Well, let us feast on your survival!" Ryan said.

The three kids sat down at their table, Aria was just fine eating the food but when she got thirsty she didn't know what to do. Slowly approaching, Professor Burton had been standing beside her.

"I brewed this tea myself, I figured you might be a little worried about what to drink. I hope this makes you feel a little better," he said, handing her the drink.

"Professor, thank you. Do you think we could start training again tomorrow? I have plans for dinner away from the school," Aria asked after she gave him a hug.

"Of course, but are you sure it's safe for you to be away from the school right now?" he asked.

"Well I assume Nona thinks I'm dead, and if anything she'd come here to figure that out, so yes I think it's safe," she replied.

"Alright, I will probably be on duty tonight so will you come and see me before you are off to bed?" he asked.

"Yes. Of course, and thanks again for the tea," Aria told him.

"My pleasure," he replied.

Aria had signaled the professor to lean in closer to her for a moment so she could whisper something in his ear, so that no one else could hear.

"I thought it was the school that made me feel safe, which it does, but I have come to realize that it's always been you, professor," she said.

Professor Burton had given her an intense look, with a side smile. At that moment he had realized that the day he would tell Aria she is his daughter, was approaching.

"After lunch, may we talk, professor?" she asked.

"Of course," he replied.

"Alright well I will meet you outside after then," she said.

Aria turned around and continued to drink her tea. She felt so relieved that Professor Burton showed up when he did. She was eager to give her thanks. She finished her meal while talking to Ryan and Reggie about her future plans to go to dinner with Nuri. Finally lunch ends and Aria goes to meet Professor Burton in the hallway.

"You wished to see me?" Professor Burton said.

"Yes. I think Professor Bliss is working for my father, and before you say anything I just want you to keep in mind how many times I have been right since I have come here. I mean, she would have had no other reason to come after me. She never knew me?" Aria stated.

"Aria something very traumatic happened to you, are you sure you're not just looking for an answer to make yourself feel better?" Professor Burton questioned.

"Are you kidding me? You're really going to say that to me right now?" she replied.

"Aria I'm sorry," he replied.

"You know what, I think I'll finish my training with Nuri and Professor Longtail. Thanks for nothing. I should have never said anything to you. I have been nothing but loyal and honest to you and it took me a lot to say this to you and you just undermine me. I thought our relationship was built on more than trust but I guess I was wrong wasn't I?" Aria replied, and walked away.

The next thing on Aria's agenda was to go see the headmaster about continuing her training with him.

The headmaster has always trusted in her theories so this was one of her last resorts. She gets to his office and knocks on the door, but he is not there. Aria then goes to look for him in the hospital wing, for her intuition is very on point. She goes in and their eyes meet.

"Hi professor, can we talk?" she asks.

"Of course, what's going on?" Professor Longtail replied.

"I want to continue my training with you, and Nuri, not the professor. Can you please help me with it? I'm almost finished and it wouldn't take too much out of your time." Aria begged.

"I would be amused to assist you with this, but why not Professor Burton? Has he done something to you?" he asks.

"Yes, in fact he has. I told him that I think Nona Bliss is working for my father and he just shut down my idea. He didn't even think to put a little trust in me. You guys are always talking about how I am a powerful witch, but when that truly matters it seems nobody but you will listen, maybe you're the only one to see my potential. I don't know. Please professor?" Aria asked again.

"Of course, we can start tomorrow between lunch and dinner, does that work for you?" he asked.

"Of course," Aria replied.

"How have you been feeling Aria, powers still intact?" Professor Steven asked.

"Yes sir, but I must go now, lots to do," Aria replied.

Aria traveled to a beautiful place in the woods next to the school. She wanted to find the perfect place for her and Nuri. As she's walking down a path to find the perfect spot she hears a faint voice calling out to her name. She doesn't understand where it's coming from and starts to walk faster hoping to find the person. Slowly a bright light shines before her.

"Darling… you look so beautiful, so talented," the faint voice says.

"Who's there?" Aria shouts while trying to hide her eyes from the blinding light.

"It's me babygirl," Sarah says.

"Mom?" Aria questions

"Yes darling. I love you so much. Don't let anyone doubt you, my child. You have such a long road ahead, you will need your strength and confidence," Sarah replied.

"Mom? Do you know who hurt me?" Aria asked.

"Yes darling. I must go now, I don't have a lot of time. Listen to your professor darling please. I love you so so much. I will always be with you," Sarah said.

Before Aria could get another word in, the bright light started to dim more and more. As the light had fully disappeared it revealed the best spot to have dinner with Nuri. Aria decided it was time to head back to the school. She wanted to talk to Professor Burton about what happened, but wasn't sure if she could trust him with the information. As soon as Aria got back to the school she went to her room to change into an outfit she looks beautiful in, but can also defend herself. Magic hidden pockets which were perfect for her. She put some money into one of the pockets and continued to walk to the back of the school from the inside. She ignored everyone that looked, or tried to speak to her including Professor Burton. He had wondered why she looked so different. She got to the back courtyard and snapped her fingers.

"About time, I was beginning to think this was never going to happen," Nuri said.

Aria sighed.

"We have a lot to catch up on," Aria replied.

"Well hop on and let's go," Nuri said.

"Okay, but we do have just one little pitstop to make," Aria said.

"And where would that be?" Nuri rolled his eyes knowing what she was up to.

"Well I brought some money along, I want to go to the Wizard Market. I haven't been there since I was a kid. I want some new clothes and I should probably buy a new wand," Aria said.

Nuri took Aria to the market and she had possessed what she needed, or wanted. After such had taken place she had finally taken Nuri to the spot where her mom showed her.

"Nuri, I saw my mom right here earlier today. She's the one who showed me this amazing spot, so cheers to her." Aria said.

"Cheers? I would but there is nothing to eat or to drink. I'm starving Aria, please do your thing already," Nuri asked.

"Okay, okay, I'm going. It's time to test out this beautiful bright silver wand of mine," Aria said.

Aria gives her wand a toss and out comes some perfect cooked chicken.

"I know you want it," as she waved it in front of his nose.

She put the chicken down for Nuri and now it was time for her to decide what she wanted for dinner. She waved her wand once more and some perfectly cooked pasta. Just the way she liked it.

"Oh my gosh Nuri, this is so good. How's your chicken?" she asked.

Nuri was a little too busy with his mouth full to be able to answer Aria, but that was enough of an answer for her.

"Can I ask you something Nuri?" Aria asked.

"Go for it," he replied.

"Well when I first created you, you said I would only be able to understand you some of the time, but I have been able to talk to you with almost every encounter we have had. Why?" she asked.

"Well, I am part of you. The more you doubt yourself, the less I become, starting with my communication. So from what I can tell you're pretty confident most of the time, especially when you are with me. It gives me ease to know you feel safe with me although I am you," Nuri replied.

"Has anyone else in the magic world created an animal with their own soul before?" Aria asked.

"I doubt it, but it is possible. Probably not an animal as big as me I'm sure," Nuri replied.

"If someone were to hurt you or even kill you, does that mean part of my soul would die?" Aria asked.

"No, not necessarily. This part of your soul would just push itself back into your body. It works differently for different situations you could potentially put yourself in Aria, but I suggest you be careful and I will as well. If it comes to where I would die, you could recreate me with the same part of your soul, but I would have no memories from the previous time you created me. I cherish our memories so I tend to keep safe." Nuri replied.

"Thanks Nuri. I'll have to make you a little girlfriend someday after the battle with my father," Aria said.

It had become very late very fast, which Aria wasn't aware of.

"We better go, I bet it's getting late. Just drop me in the back of the school once again," Aria told Nuri.

They started to head back to the school, Nuri dropped Aria off as quietly as he could.

"I love you, stay safe Nuri," Aria said as he got ready to lift off.

Aria walked back into the school not realizing the sun was almost about to come up. She had almost reached her room, but then all of a sudden she hears someone behind her.

"Aria?" Professor Longtail said.

"Professor Longtail? It's quite interesting to find you on this side of the school at such an hour," Aria replied.

"Well most of the staff had to wake up early today and keep an eye out for you. You hadn't returned last night, and we weren't sure if that was your doing, or someone else's" he replied.

"What, like my father? Professor Bliss? Nobody cared what I had to say about that so they shouldn't care whilst I'm not here either. Professor Burton knew I was leaving last night, I told him before I decided to take a break from him," Aria said.

"Yes I understand, but you hadn't come back and it's already six in the morning, but I'm sure you were aware of that?" Professor Longtail asked.

"It's already six in the morning!" Aria asked.

"Yes, but Aria, I know you're not technically a student here just yet, but our rules still apply to you. You're still a child and you wanted to stay here which means you are our responsibility. Please in the near future, be careful and you need to be here at night," he said.

"Yes, I take full responsibility, I had no idea it was that late. I was with Nuri, my Nuri. We had a picnic and then just talked for hours, I'm sorry. Can we still train later today?" Aria asked.

"If you're still awake, by all means," Professor Longtail replied.

Aria went to her room and slept until lunch time. In the meantime the headmaster thought it would be a good idea to let Professor Burton know that Aria was in fact alright.

"Professor, a word please?" Longtail said.

"Is she alright? Have we found her?" Burton asked.

"Yes, everything is alright. She was with Nuri and they had a picnic and talked, I guess they must have just lost track of time. What's going on with you two? Why am I training with her today instead of you?" Longtail asked.

"She thinks Nona is working for her so-called father, but you saw what happened in the woods and how jealous she was acting," Burton said.

"Professor, I don't think she did this to Aria over you. I have to say I agree with Aria. Every day that goes by is closer to the day she needs to go see her father, and every day that goes by that she doesn't train puts her more at risk for not being able to come back. Don't you want Aria to be able to come home and find out that she didn't just murder her own father?" Longtail asked.

"I'll try to talk to her," Burton said.

"I would still like to train with her today, and you will not only talk to her, you will apologize. Courage and honesty is a two way street professor," Longtail says as he walks away slowly, and greets the children good morning.

The time for Aria's training finally arrives and she meets the headmaster in the courtyard. Surprised, she sees Ryan and Reggie as well. She's hoping she's not walking into a lecture.

"What are you guys doing here? I missed you," Aria said.

"We're here to help you train. Figured you could use some friendly faces around while you practice since you're fighting with Professor Burton right now," Ryan said.

"Thanks and we're not fighting, I'm just disappointed in him for not trusting me. Let's get to it,"

"Are you all ready?" Longtail asked.

"Yes sir," all the children said.

"Aria, stand over there, and Ryan you stand right here. Now, the most common way to fight in the magic world is dueling. Even the wise wizards and witches use this method. I understand Professor Burton has already briefed you on how to do this as I have with Ryan. Take out your wands and get them ready. 3, 2, 1," Longtail said.

Both Aria and Ryan take out their wands and on the count of three they start the dueling.

"Delictum," Aria shouts.

As they start to duel Professor Longtial continues to speak.

"Now, you will notice each of the spells you have casted are different colors. Aria yours is green and Ryan yours is purple. This represents the spell you used. Do either one of you know how to end a duel or break a duel?" he asks.

All of a sudden Aria waves her wand and breaks the duel.

"Very good, Professor Burton has been teaching you well," Longtail said.

"Well I may have to kill my father so I hope so," Aria remarked.

"What I wanted you to notice the most was the pressure you felt whilst dueling. I want you to remember that the stronger your opponent, the more pressure you're going to feel. Now, do you know what to do if your opponent is stronger than you, Aria?" Longtail asked.

"No," she said.

"If that should happen with your father your best bet is going to be to cast him without dueling as much as you can. It will be difficult because your father knows he is stronger than you, so he knows dueling is most likely the quickest way to defeat you. There is only one thing left for me to teach but I need Aria alone for this one, thanks for your assistance you two. Take the next two periods off," Longtail offered.

"See you later! Come sit with us at dinner," Ryan said and hugged Aria.

"What's up professor?" Aria said.

"You need to be brave. Have courage. Do not quit easily. Your father is going to talk down to you. He will come after your mind, he will be mean and nasty and may even try to bewitch you. Do not let him in. You have far too much potential to let a wizard who doesn't deserve the position, to undermine you. No one deserves the position. I don't really care what you and Professor Burton are going through. Fix it. He has your best interest at heart and has his reasons for thinking what he thinks, as well as you do. If you want him to respect you, then you need to show him you respect his thoughts as well. Understand?" Longtail demanded aggressively.

"Yes. I'll do my best. I guess I never looked at it like that. Thank you professor," Aria said.

"Good, dinner is in thirty minutes, I hope you'll be there," Longtail said.

Aria thought about what she might say to Professor Burton. She felt bad for being the reason for their distance especially after he stayed up all night worried sick about her. Finally she went into the dining room to find everyone in their seats ready to eat. Aria walked past Ryan and Reggie and sat at the professors table once again. She plopped down right next to Professor Burton.

"Hey, I'm sorry. You have your reasons for thinking she isn't working with my father, and I have my reasons for thinking that she is. I just wanna put this behind us, perhaps agree to disagree?" Aria whispered to the professor whilst looking straight forward.

"I agree with you Aria. I worked with her for so long at this school. I guess I'm just very disappointed and I'm sorry as well. Go sit with your friends, we're all good here," he replied.

Aria then got up and went and sat with Reggie and Ryan.

"What was all that about?" Reggie said.

"We got into a disagreement but it's all okay now. No worries," Aria replied.

They continued to eat their dinner until they were no longer hungry.

"Hey, do you guys think I've waited too long? Should I already have fought my father?" Aria asks.

"Absolutely not. You're an amazing witch don't mind me, but Aria you barely knew anything when you first came here. I think it's good that you stuck around to learn more about magic cause he probably would have killed you," Reggie said.

"Yeah I have to be honest Aria I agree with my brother," Ryan agreed.

"Well I guess that's a good thing," Aria said.

Time does its thing and the students all get ready for bed.

"Professor Burton. I may have an idea I believe you will favor," William said.

"What's that?" Burton said.

"Well, seeing that Aria likes to make herself known as a night owl, I say we keep her up tonight, she can patrol with you and I during which we can each get to know her on a deeper level," William suggested.

"That would be amazing. Should I go tell her?" Burton asked.

"Actually let me do it. I will take the first shift," William replied.

Professor Longtail then goes to Aria's room hoping she hadn't already snuck out once again. He quickly made his way to her private room. Finally he knocked on the door twice, and Aria opened it immediately.

"What's going on professor?" she asked.

"Well Professor Burton and I know just how much you like to be up at night and wanted to know if you would like to help us patrol tonight. Him and I need to switch shifts every two hours, and you could just switch between him and I?" William asked.

"Of course, I was probably going to sneak out anyway. My sleep schedule is a little messed up at the given moment," Aria replied.

"I figured as much. Alright well I'm on first so let us get started," William said.

"Okay great. Are there really any people out at this hour, you know after lights out?" Aria asked.

"Not without getting in trouble," Professor Longtail replied.

The professor and Aria had talked the entire two hours of their shift. Aria had shared things about herself that she never thought she would have, as well as the professor. Aria never imagined having a relationship as such with an educator, but she was so grateful to have what she did. The start of Professor Burton's shift had finally begun. For Aria it had felt like not a second had passed.

"I think we had a fulfilling time, alas it is time for me to hand you over to Professor Burton," William said.

"Thank you, I really do appreciate all this professore," Aria replied.

Professor Burton and Aria started to wander the castles corridors.

"How was your time with Professor Longtail?" Professor Burton asked.

"It was really nice. We talked a lot and I feel like I may know him quite better now. I have something to talk to you about. I think the time is pretty close. I feel after another day at the school I should go see my father. Of course I will say all my goodbyes, on account for having a last day at school," Aria stated.

"Are you sure it's the right time? I will support you no matter what, but I want your head to be straight when you depart from us," Professor Burton asked.

"Yes I believe so. Nuri thinks I'm ready as well. He wants to help me but I told him no. I couldn't bear to see him hurt. I'm going to need a lot of trust and support through this, and I know you've been more of a father figure than my real dad, are you sure you can handle it?" Aria questioned.

"Since you have come to this school have you ever seen me not able to handle a tough situation?" Professor Burton remarks.

"I guess you're right. If I'm going to have enough time to say goodbye to everyone I think I should get some sleep. It'll probably be a good day to be up early," Aria giggles.

Aria slowly makes her way to her room, collecting her thoughts and trying to come to an understanding that in two days she will once again see her father. She wonders what she will think and feel in the moment. She wondered how the situation would end. Would he be dead? Would she be dead? Aria was nervous but the adrenaline rush she got from that excitement is what fed her to continue on.

"Unlimited possibilities," Aria thought to herself.

Aria finally arrived at her room. She put all of her stuff down and started to get into her bed, but before she could she saw herself in the mirror. She slowly got back up and stood closer and closer to the mirror. Carefully examining each part of her body. Sometimes it felt like she had been living in someone else's body. She struck her cheek with the outside of her hand, and looked into her eyes. Suddenly she turned around and finally went to sleep.

The next morning the sun had risen. Aria got out of bed, got dressed, and did her beautiful long hair into a beautiful braided bun. She was just about ready to leave when she opened her door and standing there was Ryan and Reggie, along with Professor Longtail, and Burton. Aria had never had people show up for her as such. She hadn't felt loved in a long time, but seeing her friends supporting her at her toughest times changed everything.

"Morning! We got permission to eat here in the room with you. It was supposed to be breakfast in bed but you're already up and dressed. That's okay though, doesn't change how good this food is going to taste," Ryan giggled.

"We are very excited for you. Your big day is coming and we wanted you to know we're here for you. We're not your friends anymore, we're family," Reggie commented.

"I wouldn't call it so much as a 'big day' but I love this thank you guys. Professor, thank you," Aria stated.

"Oh, did you think we weren't going to be joining you? This is a big day child, all four of us are part of this surprise, but seeing you are awake and on the go, I say we have breakfast outside away from the other students eh?" Professor Longtail asks.

"Of course, it's a bit chilly out there no?" Aria asked.

"Yes, so get your jacket," Professor Burton instructed.

The five of them continued into the garden in the back of the school. Being in a school full of witches and wizards they could control the temperature in just about any room with a simple flick of their wand. Aria steps into the garden and sees the most delicious looking breakfast she had seen since she's been at the school. They all devour their food.

"May I ask if you are nervous, Miss. Whitlock?" William asked.

"A little, but honestly I'm ready for whatever the outcome may be. Whether I win or lose, at least I did my best. I trained really hard with all of you. I truly believe that good will always triumph over bad, so if I do lose something good will come out of it," Aria replied.

For the rest of the day Ryan, Reggie, and Aria fly their way through the castle and outside in the cold. Snow had not yet fallen, for it had only been October, but it had surely felt like it. Aria liked the chilly fall air. The day had been so perfect for Aria, but she wanted to take care of one last thing before she would rest her head and leave to see her father in the morning. She strolled around the school, visually accepting all of the decorations, and seeking for Professor Burton. Aria believed that love was a stronger action than it was a word. She eventually found him speaking to the headmaster, ran up to him and gave him a giant hug. So heartfelt the professor started to tear up.

"What's this for?" Burton had asked.

Aria had said nothing, hoping to make a true statement, and walked away to her room. As she was undoing her hair, and changing out of her clothes, it started to click more and more.

"Tomorrow is basically today," she thought to herself.

As nervous as she was she knew this was the first step in her journey to becoming a great witch, especially for her age. As young as they come. She had laid her head down, closed her eyes, and went to sleep.

"Until tomorrow," she muttered.

The following day, she woke up and got dressed. She took everything she would need for a fight. Aria tends to travel quite lightly. She planned to have breakfast with her friends once more before she left. She knew her father was eager to find her, and did not want to keep him waiting.

"Wow, I'm going to miss you so much Aria. You better come back and start school!" Ryan said.

"Yeah, we'll always have room for you here. Please come back," Ryan agreed.

"I am going to do my best. Like I said guys, I'm ready for whatever the outcome is. I got a really good sleep, and I'm here eating with you guys. I feel like everything will be okay," Aria replied.

Breakfast goes by quickly and Nuri is waiting out in the front of the school for Aria. All of the school follows her out the door. She gets herself onto Nuri with Professor Burton's assistance.

"Wish me luck, let's go babe," Aria said.

Aria started to ride away, the image of her got smaller and smaller the further away she got.

"Luck," Professor Burton said with his head towards the ground.

Aria went back to the spot where she first discovered she could speed travel.

"Okay Nuri, I think this is your stop. I think you'll know if I need your help. I love you Nuri. If I die and you for some reason stay alive, I want you to go back to the school and be a companion for my friends and for the other Nuri. I love you," Aria stated.

Nuri left Aria on her own at this point. Aria raised her hands up and went to her fathers dimension. Aria confidently and slowly walked into what seemed to be an open dueling range. She stood there for about two minutes before her father was notified of her arrival. When Oliver found out, he had dropped everything he was doing to meet her out in front of the prison.

"So it's true? You have come back to your papa!" Oliver said.

Oliver was expecting some kind of response. He assumed Aria would be heart broken after everything she's been through. He thought she'd have many questions, but he was wrong. Aria already had family elsewhere and those are the only people she cared about.

Aria struck her wand and hit Oliver in the left arm. It had gotten him angry so he struck back, but missed Aria. Spells were thrown back and forth between the two of them, but then Oliver had stopped.

"Let's take a half time break shall we? I have a little something for you that I think you may have been looking for," Oliver says.

Aria continues to stand there, a little confused about what's about to happen.

"Bring him out!" Oliver shouts at the top of his lungs.

The workers of Oliver slowly drag Collin out of the building, barely conscious.

"Collin! What's the matter with you? Do you enjoy doing this to people, father? I don't understand where you get off in all this!" Aria shouts.

"KILL HIM!" Oliver shouts.

"NO!" Aria shouts.

The workers of Oliver continue to cast a curse on Collin's soul, and he dies before Aria and her father. Oliver hearing Aria call him father did nothing but erk him to execute her as well. Oliver strikes at Aria once again, but lands her in a duel. The workers of Oliver had stood watching as this was a climatic event in magic history. Unfortunately for Aria, she couldn't stop looking at Collins' body. It had been so lifeless, so desperate. Aria eventually drops down to her knees, doing her best to maintain her strength so she doesn't lose.

Meanwhile at the school, Professor Burton and Professor Longtail had been chatting in Professor Longtail's office. Suddenly, Professor Burton gets a slight tingle in his head.

"Oh my," he says.

"What-What is it, did she lose?" William asks.

"She needs help, fast. I'm leaving now," Burton says.

Professor Burton goes as fast as he can. He runs out of the school and into the woods. As he can also speed travel. He gets there relatively quickly. He can hear the duel from just a small distance away. He finds his way to each of them to find Aria still on her knees fighting as hard as she possibly could. He runs out of the bushes and blasts Oliver back, making him fall onto the ground, and his crew flee.

"Aria!" Professor Burton says.

"Professor Burton!? What are you doing here? You need to leave, now! They killed Collin!" Aria shouts and cries.

"I'm not going anywhere," he replies.

"That's probably a good thing. I think now would be a wonderful time to finally tell Aria the truth, don't you think?" Oliver asked.

"What the bloody hell is talking about?" Aria asked.

"Aria, I-" Burton is cut off.

"Your mother, dear Aria. She was a spirited one, yes she was. I remember the night before I married your mother. It's usually said that it's bad luck for the bride and groom to see each other the night before the wedding eh? I've always wondered what she did that night. Nuri! I believe that's where you come in. I want you to tell Aria what her mother did before our wedding. I want you to look her in the eye. This will be good," Oliver said.

"What's happening?" Aria said, confused.

"Look, your mother and I met a long time ago. Before she knew Oliver. We were in love, but eventually she chose him, and I had met someone else. The night before your parents wedding, you were conceived, Aria. The only thing is that Oliver isn't the one who fathered you. I am. I'm truly sorry. I was waiting for the right time to tell you. Your mother cheated on him the night before they got married, with me" Burton said.

Oliver and Burton had expected Aria's response to be a lot different than it really was.

"Well that's fine then, I'll change my name. He's been more of a father to me than you ever have. You're a real step up from Oliver. I love you, dad?" she said with anger and passion.

With a smile on his face Professor Burton strikes Oliver.

"What are you doing?" Aria asked.

"Well we still have to fight him. He's not a good man Aria," Burton said.

"Don't you realize everything that has happened? Sure he's not a good guy, but we are the good guys. He's down. Let's just take him in. Please? For your daughter?" Aria giggled and bribed.

"Alright, I will personally take him in. You can go and help the others out of their shackles. I will see you back at the school," Burton said.

Aria helped the other wizards get out of the prison and back to their long awaited families. Afterwards, she took Nuri back to the school and met up with her friends. They were all so happy to see her. It was well into the night by the time Professor Burton had finally gotten back to the school, but Aria waited up for him.

"I'm so tired," Aria said.

"Go to bed. We can discuss everything, and I mean everything, tomorrow," Burton said.

"Until tomorrow," Aria replied.